J. B. Coats, Dwight Williams

Poems and fragments in prose

J. B. Coats, Dwight Williams

Poems and fragments in prose

ISBN/EAN: 9783337374044

Printed in Europe, USA, Canada, Australia, Japan

Cover: Foto ©Andreas Hilbeck / pixelio.de

More available books at **www.hansebooks.com**

P O E M S

AND

Fragments in Prose.

BY MRS. J. B. COATS.

CINCINNATI:
WALDEN AND STOWE.
PRINTED FOR THE AUTHOR.
1881.

CONTENTS.

CONTENTS. 5

ILLUSTRATIONS.

INTRODUCTION.

THE mission of poetry is largely practical. The gift is by no means so rare as is often supposed. The field of poesy is not one whose gates are guarded by strong and frowning sentinels, who only admit the great ones wearing the insignia of wealth and position. It is a beautiful domain where all pure and loving souls may go and enjoy their day-dreams of beauty, friendship, nature, and God. Unlike the other fine arts, poetry is left to struggle much alone. Masters of painting have their pupils, whom they lead into the mysteries of outline and color. Music has its conservatories, where the mind is trained in the mathematics of quantity, where the fingers are put under the most rigid discipline, and the soul is led into the delightful mazes of harmony. The poet has less help and fewer

companions. He needs a more daring spirit, for in the
schools less provision is made for poetry than for the
other arts.

Hence the poet struggles with greater difficulties.
His must be a greater self-development. His must be
a more positive originality. Perhaps this is best.
When success is achieved it is lasting. It wins the
widest recognition.

There is not a little chivalry in the venture and ad-
venture of a gentle woman taking the path indicated in
this volume. It is a courage having its birth in a quiet
rural home, amid the loves of the household, the pres-
sure of secular duties, and the struggles of a life that
has in it the modestly heroic, for it attempts great and
beautiful results in the face of contingency and trial.

Christian love has prompted the work. It comes a
fragrant offering to a glowing altar. Our friend, Mrs.
Coats, has sung these songs from the banks of her own
charming Seneca, and in the rhythm and the rhyme are
the echoes of her beautiful surroundings. The field she
has entered is a large one. The books of poetry written
are many, but the world has need of them. The singers
all have listeners. Some of them are sad and weary.

The key-note of every pure song rings melody into some heart. The age of poetry is by no means done. The new years bring new phases of society and history, and new interpretations of nature, and wider areas of divine wisdom, power, and love. To those familiar with the songs of the authoress the volume will have a peculiar charm. The melodies go forth for a double purpose, to drop sunlight into hearts and homes, and bring material aid to the beautiful Church to whose altar the book is a fragrant and willing offering. It shall go with many a prayer, and He who gathers the bread cast upon all waters will give the effort his smile and his blessing. So we commend the work for its own sake, and the benevolent design that accompanies it.

DWIGHT WILLIAMS.

August 25, 1880.

POEMS

— AND —

FRAGMENTS IN PROSE.

The Oak and the Vine.

I AM thinking of the time
  When first I saw this tree—a little oak
Not larger round than a man's arm,
And yet it held itself in quite a lofty way,
  As if it meant to stand, even though strong
    winds should strive to lay it low.
And so we thought to plant a vine beside its
    root,
  A vine that carried in its heart a prophecy of
    purple fruit in years to come.
And so we watched the timid little thing,
And by and by we saw it lift its eyes in bashful way
  up toward the oak,
Which nodded back its welcome.

And from that day they were fast friends, and whispered to each other;
And the birds looked wise and poised their little heads
in listening way,
As if some pleasant secret, they had come to share
with them.

And so through all the Summer days
They lived their happy lives.
The oak, growing in beauty and in strength,
And reaching out its arms to meet the vine,
Which swayed and laughed in pretty and coquettish way,
Until at last its gentle fingers touched the sturdy oak,
And clasped them in a close embrace.
Henceforth their lives were joined, and to each other
they were all in all.
And so the Providence that gives the lily its fair dress
Gave to the newly-wedded pair their food from the
moist earth,
Or from the bracing air; and gave them dew to slake
their thirst,
And washed their leafy robes with frequent showers,
and blest them day by day.

And thus the years went on, no blight of sorrow marred
    their lives;
And the proud oak still prouder grew,
Lifting itself high toward the heavens,
As man, when crowned with wisdom, towers above his
    fellowmen.

Meanwhile the vine,
Made haste to wind itself, with stronger grasp, about
    the oak.
Its leaves and tendrils clinging in modest way,
Climbing to greater heights in fearless fashion,
As though it might have said,
"Where'er thou goest, I too will go."
And so the oak, perhaps unconsciously, shielded the vine,
    Its great trunk keeping off the northern blast,
While its broad crown of leaves caught the hot sun
    rays,
Which in their fullest strength might scorch the vine,
    And blast its dainty leaves—
It caught, and broke them up in little bits,
And sent them drifting, here and there, over the vine,
To warm its roots, and touch its clustered fruit with
    royal ·color.

And so it stands to-day, a pretty sight,
With wide circumference of bough and leaf,
Making an ample shade
For all the birds, that love to picnic in its depths.
Half-way around its vastness climbs the vine,
Touching the rough gray bark in a caressing way,
Or hiding in the depths of darker green;
Its tendrils floating carelessly,
Like lawless locks of hair that creep from out their
     fastenings,
And twine and ripple over girlish faces,
Or about their snowy throats.

And thus the two go to make up a perfect whole.
For the great tree, so massive and so grand,
Might have within its heart of oak
A sense of loneliness, and pain, and sorrowful unrest,
     Which presence of the vine doth heal and satisfy.
And by its help in lifting up the vine to high estate,
     And caring in such tender fashion for its weal,
     Incites the vine to friendship and lofty gratitude.
And so through coming years each one will help the
     other,

Until the habit of their lives
Will be the ruling passion in their death;
And when the oak shall cast its leaves,
And its life-pulses cease to beat,
When its great form returns to earth,
Then, like a widow in her weeds,
The vine will hang its head, and drop its gay attire,
Bowing in sorrow o'er its dead,
Yet grateful that the same broad grave,
The heart of mother earth, will shelter both.

Lines

ON PARTING WITH A DEAR FRIEND.

WHAT is the secret of the nameless grace,
That, like a *presence*, follows in her train?
Is it the witching power of voice or face
That makes us wish she soon would come again?

What makes the tender touch of her pure hand
Bring to me comfort, all my being thrill?
Is it the outgrowth of Christ's last command?
"Love one another, thus my law fulfill."

Is it her sympathy for us and ours?
   As troubles gather o'er us dense and dark,
Her helpful words have had a soothing power,
   To lift away the burden from our hearts.

Is it the love glance from her kindly eyes?
   Is it because our sorrows she would share,
And knows just how to tell them all to Christ
   In fitting words, of sweetly uttered prayer?

Whate'er the cause, we dread to say good-bye,
   For she has brought us joy in place of pain;
And so we hope the time will quickly fly,
   And bring the day when she will come again.

John on the Isle of Patmos.

PATMOS, a lonely, rugged isle,
   Barren and desolate.
   Was made the home of Christ's beloved,
Exiled for love of him who died for all—
   A life-long stain upon the sinful man
   Who, clothed with brief authority,

John on Patmos

Doomed him to loneliness for weary years,
No friend to speak to him a word of cheer;
    Naught left but precious memories
Of the dear home on Galilee's fair shore,
Of Jordan's winding stream,
And all the beauteous land made sacred
    As the home of Him who bore our sins.

    The exile's feet paced to and fro
From shore to shore of that lone isle.
Except a single palm, no vegetation met his eye;
    The sea-bird's note the only sound he heard,
    Save the dull music of the waves,
As they surged back and forth against the shore.
    Yet he was not alone,
For was he not Christ's chosen brother?
And he had cared, as only loving son could care,
    For the dear mother of our Lord.
While he kept the lonely watch
He lived again the years
    When the dear Christ walked with him
    O'er the Judean hills,
Or, in its valleys, lingered
To heal the sick, and comfort the afflicted;

To give the weeping mother back her dead,
　　Or teach earth's sorrowing ones
　　To look beyond, to the good time
When Life Eternal might be made the heritage of all.

　　When high up the mountain side
The exile sought, 'neath overhanging rock,
　　　A resting place,
His stony pillow brought to mind the time
When his head rested on the Savior's breast,
And the last words of counsel from his lips
　　Who said, "My peace I give to you."

　　　With aching heart
He lives again those sad, sad days.
He sees the form beloved dragging the heavy cross;
　　And memory, faithful to her trust,
　　Brings all the gloomy picture to his view,
Until the last, low wail from broken heart,
" It is now finished," echoed from Calvary's height.
Oh, how those words have thrilled from pole to pole,
From center to circumference of this wide earth,
　　Heralding the birth of joys uncounted
　　To all earth's repentant sons.

None but a God could have conceived
  A plan so wondrous.
And the lone exile, full of rapture at the thought,
Forgot the desolation of his home, and rested,
As only loving heart can rest, in the Beloved.

  The Sabbath hush came down,
Like benediction o'er the earth,
As John came forth to offer morning sacrifice.
  The moon's last rays,
The lines of light that spoke of day's approach,
The voices of the air and sea.
  All told him of a risen Lord.
He stands erect,
  His white locks wet with early dew,
His eyes turned heavenward,
  Seeming to wear the look
Of those pure eyes that beamed on him so long ago,
His shining face reminding one of Moses
When, from Sinai's cloud,
  He came to Israel's host.

  He says, "I, John, was in the spirit,
  And, while absorbed in worship,
A voice, like trumpet tone, came to mine ear,

And heavenly vision met mine eye,
    Like to the Christ of other days.
Yet, clothed with wondrous majesty,
His face was like the sun, shining in strength.
    A two-edged sword was in his mouth,
    And in his right hand seven stars.
His eyes like flaming fire,
His head and hair were white like wool."

John saw, and, like a dead man, fell to earth.
    Not long he lay entranced, for soon
The dear right hand was laid upon him.
    The touch thrilled every nerve
    And brought him back to life.
A voice, whose music was like many waters, said :
    " Fear not, I am alive forevermore ;
But write the things thou seest,
The things that are and shall hereafter be.
    Be thou my messenger, and,
To the angels of the seven Churches, write
    My tender counsels,
My loving thoughts of them.
    Warn them to shun all evil,
And strive to overcome,

That they may eat of life's fair tree,
And have the white stone, sign of victory."
Early in life the loved disciple learned to obey,
    And now his willing hands
Hastened to pen the words
    That fell from lips of Him
Who held the keys of life and death.
    The work complete,
And then the door of heaven was opened,
And words of invitation fell upon his ear,
    "Come hither,
I will show thee things which must hereafter be."

We may not go in spirit, as did John,
And see the throne with rainbow girt about;
Nor look upon the one who sits thereon,
Whose likeness is to jasper and to sardine stones;
    Nor can we hear the voices
Which, like lightning and like thunder,
    From the throne proceed.
We can not see the seven lamps, or crystal sea,
But while we wait and labor for the highest good,
We may, as did the four and twenty elders, cry,
    " Worthy art thou, O Lord, forevermore!"

Angel Ministry.

"He shall give His angels charge concerning thee."

ART thou traveling, sorrowing mother,
　　O'er a rough and stormy way?
　Do the cares about thee gather,
　　Growing heavier day by day?
He the precious one, the Savior,
　He who dwells enthroned in light,
Knows each trial, and each sorrow,
　And can bid them take their flight.

Tired father, do thy footsteps
　　Sometimes falter 'neath the load
Of the burdens thou art bearing,
　　O'er the straight and narrow road?
He has promised that his angels
　Shall about thy pathway stand,
And, with loving care and tender,
　Will uphold thee in their hands.

Aged pilgrim, weak and trembling,
　Under more than fourscore years,

As the shadows still enfold thee,
  Are thy cheeks bedewed with tears?
He will wipe away all sorrow,
  Lift from thee thy grief and pain,
And perchance the glad to-morrow
  Will restore thy youth again.

Little feet that have just entered
  On the pathway to the skies,
Do temptations e'er assail thee,
  And the tempests o'er thee rise?
Look to Jesus, he has promised
  All thy footsteps well to guard;
Trust his promise and obey him,
  And his love be thy reward.

Watchman on the walls of Zion,
  Clothed in panoply of light,
Do the arrows that assail thee
  Soil thy garments, dim thy sight?
Look above, for angel watchers,
  Grouped about thee every hour,
Carry tidings up to heaven,
  Bring to thee all needful power.

A Precious Memory.

HOW like a living presence are memories of the past. They come thronging about me to-day, peopling my quiet home with dear faces, breathing in my ear the music of voices which I shall hear no more until "death is swallowed up in victory." The years so full of joy, when our darling son, the "early called," was with us, have passed in review. His wondrous beauty, combined with unusual precocity and a loving, genial temper, made him the idol of our hearts. His earnest eyes seem even now to be looking into mine, as he propounds some grave question of heaven and its joys, which can only be satisfactorily answered when this "mortal shall have put on immortality."

He was early dedicated to God, as was little Samuel, and when little more than two years of age he, too, went to minister in "the temple"—not a gorgeous edifice built of hewn stone and rich in ornaments of gold, but a "house not made with hands, eternal in the heavens."

John, "the beloved," has described it as perfectly as our poor language can convey the idea, but, please God, not far away is the time when we shall know for ourselves what the "heart of man can not conceive." I, too, was stricken with disease, and went with him to the river's brink.

How I longed to go with my precious one, and lingered, listening for the summons home. In vain I waited. The little bark soon reached the other shore, while my poor aching heart tried hard to say, "It is the Lord, let him do what seemeth to him good."

The dear elder Brother came in this hour of need, and the beautiful promise, "my peace I give unto you," was measurably verified to me. I could think and talk calmly of my bereavement, and desired to feel resigned to the will of "Him who doeth all things well."

Yet one single thought perplexed me: was my darling, who had in life always been accustomed to the ministry of parents and sister, who shrank with timidity from all save the dear home faces, satisfied with the change? Did not the *strangeness* of heaven mar its perfection, to one of his delicate perceptions?

It seemed as though he must be longing for a tender father's embrace, a mother's enfolding arms, or the dear sister's songs and caresses.

During a long period of physical weakness I grew to suffer from this thought, and as I had early learned to believe in a prayer-answering God, I went to him with this mystery.

If my fledgling needed me not I could be happy in the thought that he was safe in heavenly mansions. So, in my weakness, I asked for one little sign that in heaven his happiness was unalloyed—a breath of fragrance, the rustling as of an angel's wing, the impress of his kiss upon my cheek. Thus was I answered.

My mourning is ended, and I know that when I near the "eternal hill" I shall inhale the fragrant atmosphere of my loved one's home, I shall hear the rustling of many an angel's wing, and his dear lips will again meet mine as I am led to the mansions his hands have helped to beautify.

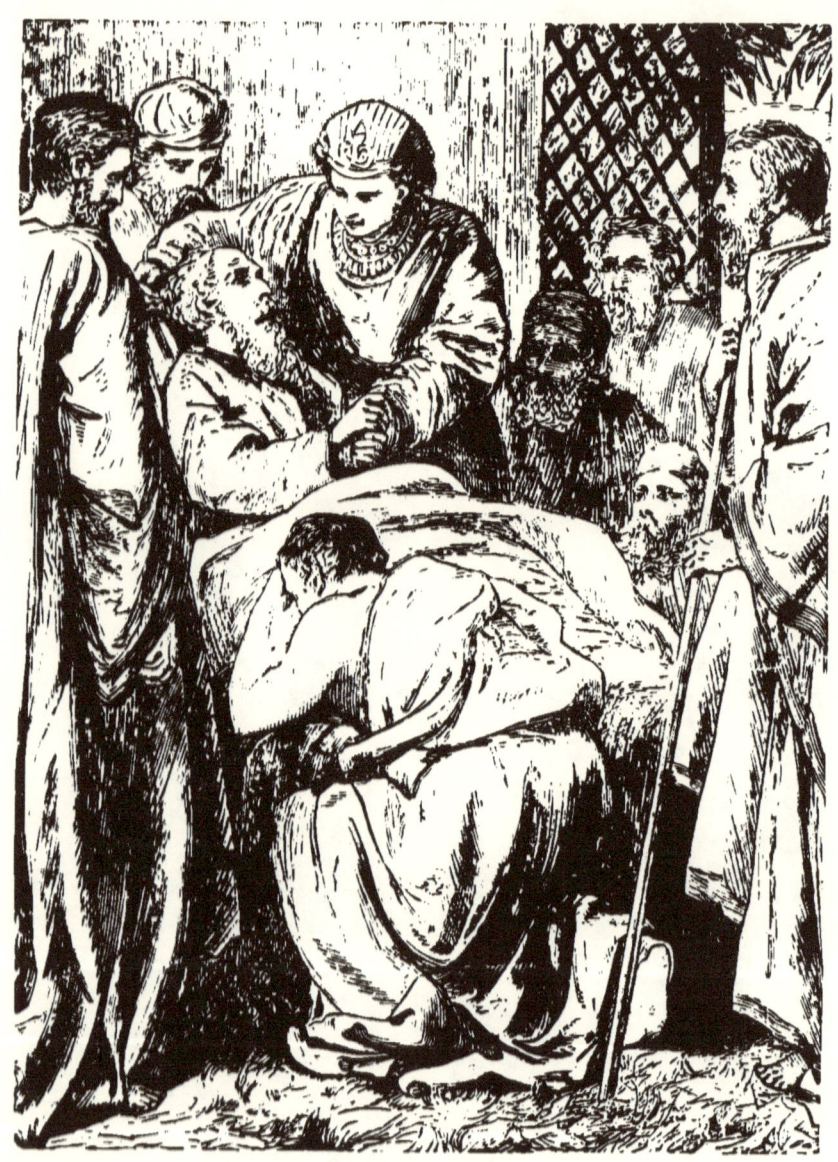

Death of Jacob.

The Death and Burial of Jacob.

JACOB, the Christian patriarch, the grand old man,
    Who loved and trusted God so fully,
        Called to his sons,—
Gather yourselves together, for behold I die;
    But God shall be with you,
And bring you to your father's land again.
Then in words prophetic he blessed each son,
But choicest blessings rested on the head of Joseph,
    Who had saved his brethren
    And his father's house
When famine, gaunt and shriveled,
Stalked through his native land.

    And Jacob charged his sons,
"Gather me unto my people,
    With my fathers bury me;"
Then gathered up his feet and yielded up the ghost.
And Joseph fell upon his father's neck
    And wept, and kissed him,
Sorrowing most that he should see his face no more,

Nor hear his words of blessing :
And he bade the servants, his physicians,
To embalm his father's body.

And the learned men of Egypt
Gathered gums and fragrant spices,
And, with skilled hands,
Applied them to the form so loved,
That they might still look on his face.

And all the brethren mourned,
And the Egyptians mourned, until the days
Three score and ten of those that are embalmed
Were all fulfilled.
After which, Joseph, the model ruler in Pharaoh's house,
Sought audience with the king,
Saying, "If now I have found grace with thee,
Hear me, I pray.
My father made me swear to lay him in the cave
Digged in Machpelah's field in Canaan,
Long since bought for burial place."
And then he told him of the kindred resting there,
And asked, "Now let me go, I pray,
And thus fulfill my vow,
And surely I will come to thee again."

Then Pharaoh bade him go,
And take with him
The servants of the king,
The elders of his house,
And all the princes of the land,
The house of Joseph and his brethren,
And his father's house,
All save the little ones, the flocks, and herds.
And with him went
Horsemen and chariots, not a few,
A great and sorrowing company.
Not all the splendors of a Pharaoh's court,
With gilded pomp, and Orient garb,
Could soothe the mourning hearts,
Save as they spoke the grief
That Israel's death had caused.

In solemn state they marched,
While memories of the good man's life
Brought comfort to their hearts,
As corn and wine of Egypt
Had brought health and strength
In those old famine days.
A long and weary pilgrimage it was,

And yet it brought some rest into their lives,
 For thus the father's dying wish was met.

   Beyond the Jordan
The sad procession halted seven days
  At threshing floor of Atad,
  And mourned a grievous mourning,
Until the dwellers in the land of Canaan said,
   " This place shall be called Abel-mizraim,
  The mourning place of Egypt's host ;"
Then onward moved to Jacob's chosen burial place,
Made sacred as the tomb of Isaac and Rebekah ;
  Abraham and Sarah, too,
Had found a resting-place within its walls,
  And Leah, wife of Jacob.

   The tomb was opened,
And the treasured form was placed within;
And, when the door was sealed,
  Joseph, the lord of Egypt,
  Knelt upon the consecrated ground
And, with his brethren,
And all the nobles, servants of his king,
  Gave thanks to Israel's God
That this, his work of love, was now complete.

And there they left
These honored sons and daughters of the living God,
To rest together, until the resurrection morn,
When they will rise, and, with united chorus, join
With patriarchs, prophets, priests, and kings,
Saying, "Salvation, glory, honor, power,
  Unto the Lord our God."

An Old Letter.

HOLD in my hand an old letter.
 'Twas written a long time ago,
And the hands that moved over the paper
 Long since were laid under the snow.

The paper—a huge sheet of foolscap—
 Is blotched and defaced by the years;
Sometimes I almost fancy
 That I see the traces of tears.

The letters are large and well-shapen;
 O'er margin and border they spread;
The heart that prompted the letter,
 Was mourning over its dead.

In his fresh, young manhood, the writer
  Had chosen a lovely bride,
And it seemed as if all the future
  Would be bright if she walked by his side.

For a few short months she tarried,
  Bringing comfort and rest to his home,
And then the dear hands were folded,
  Henceforth he must journey—*alone.*

Then his heart turned toward his young brother,
  Gifted, and loving, and true,
And he willed to bury old sorrows.
  Tried hard to begin life anew.

The love was returned in large measure,
  As when David and Jonathan loved,
The two souls in sympathy woven,
  The covenant sanctioned above.

But the old grief was deep and abiding;
  So stricken was that manly form,
That he shivered at sight of her tombstone,
  And friends ceased to mention her name.

He walked forth enshrouded in sorrow,
  No light found its way through the gloom,
The sun rays were powerless to cheer him,
  His heart found no rest, but the tomb.

    .

At last he left the old hearthstone,
  Friends feared, with reason dethroned;
No tidings, no signs did he leave them,
  But went out a wanderer, alone.

  .   .   .   .

They waited, and ceased not to pray
  That the years would restore him again,
And the dear young brother, each day
  Remembered his burden and pain.

· But time moved apace and the child-brother grew,
  And took up the work of life,
And he asked God to help and anoint him anew
  For the labor, the toil, and the strife.

His earnest prayer a prophecy proved,
  For his heart was illumined with light;
The armor of faith he buckled on,
  Made God's service his greatest delight.

He studied the Word and sought souls to win,
  And told of Christ's power to save
His friends and neighbors from paths of sin,
  And darkness, beyond the grave.

But there came a time, a sorrowful time,
  ˙When disease, with its pitiless train,
Came and bound the strong man and laid him aside,
  To battle with suffering and pain.

Loving hands were outstretched to soothe and bless,
  Loving hearts were o'er burdened with grief,
And prayers were offered for help and rest,
  That Christ would send speedy relief.

But the dear Father thought to take him home,
  Away from the toil and the care.
He cheerfully went, for Christ had gone
  Before him, the way to prepare.

A chaplet they wove and placed on his brow,
  And strong men wept bitter tears ;
The wife and children wondered how
  They could live on through the years.

Months slipped away and this letter came—
    'Twas penned in a distant clime;
The writing was strange, and only the name
    Made us think of the dear old time

When the brothers sat by the bright hearth-fire,
    Ere the blight of sorrow came,
And we knew, as we read through the blinding tears,
    That the lost was found again.

He told of the time when his early grief
    Had turned his heart to stone;
Of the blackness of night that o'er him spread,
    As he trod life's path alone.

Tender the words he spoke beside,
    Of the nobleness and truth
Of the bright young boy who, by his side,
    Had walked in the days of his youth;

Rejoiced that his manhood was crowned with grace,
    And the souls he had sought to win,
As polished jewels would shine at last,
    Cleansed, purified from sin.

At last his pen grew eloquent,
   As he spoke of redeeming power,
Of the love that sought and comforted him,
   In that fearful trial hour;

The tender touch and needful help
   Of the dear Christ-crucified,
Who lifted him out from the depths of woe,
   And gave him a place by his side;

The assurance of rest when the day was done,
   Of union with brother and friend,
A welcome to heaven from Father and Son,
   Where brightness and peace ne'er shall end.

  .   .   .   .   .

More than threescore years have passed since then,
   And the writer has gone to his rest,
Where Christ doth abide, and the mansions and crown,
   And the friends that in youth he loved best.

Prayer During Battle.

FROM THE GERMAN.

ATHER, I cry to thee,
Enveloped in smoke, 'mid roar and rattle,
Darting lightning flashes through the battle—
Guide of battles, I cry to thee;
Father, do thou lead me.

Father, do thou lead me
To victory or death, lead by thy hand,
O master, I recognize thy command;
Master, as thou wilt so lead me;
God, I recognize thee;

God, I recognize thee,
In the Autumnal rustling of heather,
So in the thunder of battle weather;
Fountain of grace, I recognize thee;
Father, do thou bless me.

Father, do thou bless me,
Into thy hands my own life I commend.
It thou hast given, in strife it may end;

Bless in life, or in death bless me;
Father, I praise thee.

Father, I praise thee;
It is no combat for fortunes of earth;
We protect with the sword truths loved from our birth.
If victorious, praise I thee;
God, commend I myself to thee.

God, commend I myself to thee,
Though the thunder of death my ear shall greet;
Should my life-blood flow, and my heart cease to beat;
God, commend I myself to thee;
My Father, I cry to thee.

Apple Blossoms.

THE air was full of sweetness,
For May, the month of bloom,
Was throwing, with lavish hand, her treasures far
and wide.
And while I longed to run away from work and care,
To watch the opening bud and springing flower,
One came, with loving thought intent,

And brought to me
Clusters of apple blossoms, pearly white,
And other groups of buds unopened, with tinge of pink,
As if the lips of morn
Had touched them with its rosy flush.
And so my heart was glad,
Glad for the charm of bud and flower,
Glad for the love that placed them in my hand.

Later I wandered forth to see the tree
From which the dainty gift was plucked;
And it was wonderful,
Like a great crown of drifting, shimmering light,
Lifting high up, and stretching far toward north and
south,
Toward eastern sky, and sunset glow,
Its graceful branches
Seeming as if it might give shade and comfort
To half a hundred hungry hearts.
And as I waited, a merry group
Came trooping up, three roguish girls.
And how they did rejoice, and clap their hands,
At sight of so much beauty;

Ran and shouted,
As they made haste to pluck
The great white balls of bloom and pelt each other,
Or wove them into garlands, far more tasteful
Than the golden crowns that princes wear.
And the old tree smiled down upon them,
As its rain of snowy leaves
Fell over floating locks of gold and brown,
As though an unseen hand
Were strewing blessings o'er their heads.

Children's Picnic.

SAYS the dear elder sister to Jennie and Fan,
Make haste with your lessons, for I have a plan;
When the tasks are all ended, we'll get mother
to say
That we children may have a picnic to-day.

Away to the garden where Summer fruits grow,
With baskets in hands let us hasten to go;
I am sure we shall find that the berries are ripe,
As well as the currants both red, black, and white.

The raspberry bushes stand guard near the gate,
All marshaled in line under orders to wait ;
They are tastefully dressed, though without shoulder-
    straps,
And in uniform style, for they all wear caps.

Yet they differ in taste, for some caps are white,
While others wear red, just as pretty a sight ;
Still others think they'll not dress like the rest,
And insist that black becomes them the best.

As they seem happy to have their own way,
It will hardly be needful for us to stay ;
And, after we've gathered a share of the fruit,
We'll give and receive a parting salute.

Next the ripe cherries so juicy and sweet,
Good for the birds, good for children to eat ;
The great black Tartarian is fit for a queen,
And the dainty white cherry, no better is seen.

Beside them is a tree of the famous ox-heart,
And the old-fashioned cherries with just enough tart ;
They delight the heart of matron and maid,
They make the best pies that ever were made.

But the birds seem inclined to have a share,
And as there is plenty, and some to spare,
We'll invite them to come, they will not refuse,
And make them quite welcome to whatever they choose.

The gooseberries claim our attention also,
For side by side with the currants they grow;
They are right royal berries, toothsome, and grand,
For gooseberry tarts, or to eat out of hand.

The strawberry vines have earned a long rest,
Their great luscious berries, the nicest and best,
Were gathered last week, and made into jam,
Packed in bowls, and in cups, and in cans.

We'll spread our feast in the arbor wide,
In the coolest place, on the shady side,
Where the sunbeams quiver through the leaves,
And the shadows play among the trees.

We'll trip along through tangles of vines,
That in their self-will refuse to twine
Over the frames in an orderly way,
But hide in the grasses and wander away.

We'll dance to the music of birds and of bees,
On the velvety carpet, that dear nature weaves;

As happy as fairies, in innocent play,
For our hearts will be full of delight all the day.

We'll fashion a swing 'neath the willow's shade,
Of woven grape-vines it shall be made;
We'll have a broad seat that shall hold two or three,
Cushioned with mosses the seat shall be.

We'll have a gay time the whole afternoon,
And the dews will be falling for us far too soon;
But we'll try to be good, and one month from to-day
We may possibly have another play-day.

Whole races of plums with their cousins and friends,
Will greet you by scores, by hundreds, by tens;
Their wardrobe, so varied with green, blue, and gold,
That you'll almost wonder, "can they ever grow old?"

The great golden peaches will try to abide
'Neath clusters of leaves, their blushes to hide;
Yet to make children happy is part of their plan,
So they shrink not from touch of a little soft hand.

And thus the late spring-time has fruits of its own,
And when golden sunshine of Summer shall come
Its fruitage reminds us of God's promise given,
Of the rainbow he wrought, and hung in the heavens.

The Death of a Neighbor.

THE dear old man,
  So ripe in years, so rich in goodness,
    Who through all his later life
Has garnered treasures for the better land,
        Is ready to depart.
His fourscore years have been well spent,
For he loved God, and loved to do his will;
He loved the house of prayer,
        Where he found strength and help.
A Bethel was his closet,
Where his soul was fed each day with heavenly bread.
        He loved the souls of men,
And sought to win them to the higher life.
The Word of God was dear to him;
Its precious truths like unto household words,
Which made his daily speech a benediction to other
        hearts.
And now his days are nearly run,
He lays his armor by, he needs it not;
His battles are all fought, his victories are complete;

And quietly he says,
"The time of my departure is at hand;
No fear have I, for I have kept the faith,
And He, whose word is sure, has said,
Henceforth there is a crown laid up for me,
A crown of righteousness, which God the Judge,
Shall give me at the last."
And holding fast the word which held the promise
Of the resurrection of the just, he died,
        Laying aside the flesh
As ripened ears burst from their husky covering,
Which falls to earth,
        While the ripe grain is garnered
As a prophecy of fuller life in time to come.
        And when God wills
The worn and tired frame which yielded to the power
    of death   .
Shall all be changed, and newly wrought,
And clothed with health eternal,
Yet with familiar smile and glance
        To cheer immortal eyes
That knew him in the flesh.

Seneca Lake.

THOU loveliest of all the lakes,
　　We fain would speak thy praise ;
　　　　But much we fear
That fitting words we may not find
To clothe the thoughts that come to us.
　　We know thou art beloved,
　　　For when we journey from thy side
We miss thy presence, as if some pleasant thing
Had slipped away and left us in unrest until restored
　　　again.
And so in early morn we seek thy face,
Perchance to see thee veiled in mist,
　　　　Which might be
Breath of prayer, or praise from thy great heart
　　　Ascending towards the heavens.
　　Or yet again we see thee restful, placid,
The drifting clouds reflected in thy depths,
As if an answered prayer were nestling there.

And thou art beautiful at close of day,
　　　When shadows fall aslant,

Touching the farther shore;
Revealing light and shade, and golden gleam,
And silver sheen, and broken rays,
And bars of light, in almost every hue,
As if a passing rainbow had been charmed,
  And lingered for a time,
As lovers linger, to watch the changing face,
Or listen to the music of the voice most dear.

  We love thee in thy quiet moods,
For thou dost prophesy of peace and rest;
'Tis then we best can read thy thoughts,
  And listen to the tales of olden time,
  When silence reigned supreme.
We marvel much at all the knowledge
Thou hast gained of nations that have lived and died;
Of other secrets thou hast kept for centuries,
Sealed secrets, till the waters
  Yield their treasures up.
We know that thou couldst tell us
  Of thy wondrous depths,
  That line or plummet can not sound,
And of the living tribes that dwell so far beneath,
That human eye ne'er rested on their homes.

We dare not peer into thy hidden mysteries,
        But love to hear thy voice
        Discoursing of such things
        As may be right for us to know.
And surely we may talk to thee, and thou to us,
Of all the beauteous things that gird thee round
    (Most fitting setting for such royal gem);
            Of rocks,
        And hills, and emerald slopes,
        Of quiet groves, and waterfalls,
Far reaching pastures, broken up by tiny silver threads,
    That wander down to find their way
            Into thy life.

        We know the glens and gorges,
        With their strange wild beauty,
Through which come tidings of the world beyond,
            Are dear to thee;
        And we know, too, that thou art happy,
        In changes wrought from day to day,
            As nature puts on seasonable dress,
            Laying aside her wintry robe
            To don the pretty garb of Spring,
Made up in daintiest device, and colors rare.

Later, to be exchanged
For trailing Summer garments, made in
Richer tints, with draping exquisite,
Of vine and leaf, which please and satisfy;
Until at last the Autumn comes, with stately tread,
Bringing such wealth of color,
That it seems that all the earth has brought
Its tributes to her feet;
And, with a quiet dignity, she moves about,
Touching each tree or shrub
With gold or scarlet flame,
With brown or russet,
Or with brushes dipped in royal purple dyes,
Until thou art so clothed about,
That if one looked o'er all the earth,
A lovelier spot might not be found.

Thou art of life a type,
And so we sympathize in all thy moods.
Sometimes fierce winds assail,
As if to test thy strength,
And storms beat hard, and bring to thee distress;
And thou art wearied with the strife,

4

And dost call forth thy hidden forces,
Who come in legions and battalions,
In wrath and foam,
As if their fury would not be appeased.
Even in the voice of battle
Thou art grand, for we are sure
A guiding Hand will hold thy rage,
And that thy bounds are set.
And when the Voice that rules the world
Shall bid thy waves, "Be still," thou wilt obey.
And so in storm or calm,
Thou tellest us of Him, "whose way is in the sea,
Whose path leads through the waves,
Whose footsteps are not known."

A Mother's Prayer.

IT was in early morning of a year long gone,
A mother's voice was pleading for a precious son;
Dear Father, wilt thou bless and save our only one!

The mother's heart was aching with its dread and fears,
She asked God for wisdom to help her through the years,
Her voice was low and sweet and full of unshed tears.

She did not ask that he in wealth or fame should share,
But asked that he might lead a life of prayer,
And if it pleased God, he that life would spare

To be henceforth a chosen blessing to his race,
And while he talked with God as face to face,
Teach others how like precious faith to embrace.

Angels with pitying heart were hovering near,
And the dear Savior kindly lent his ear
And heard her prayer, and counted every tear.

Time hastened on, the mother's heart was stayed
By loving care of Him, whom gladly she obeyed,
For in His hands her burden had been laid.

Later the blessed hour of triumph came
When he, the son she loved, rose to proclaim
Redeeming grace, undying love, through Jesus' name.

And then of good old Simeon's faith she thought,
Praised God for mercies that his hand had wrought,
That through shed blood redemption had been bought;

Thought of that sad morning, all its grief and pain;
Thought of the tears that fell like Summer rain,
And of God's promise, "I will come again."

And he had come in such abounding love,
Bringing the best gift from the courts above
And laid it on her heart, His peace, the blessed dove.

A Memorial.

SPENDING a little time in the home of a friend, a
bereaved mother, our thoughts and words naturally
drifted to our "treasures in heaven;" for although
many years had passed since our darling son "was not,
for God took him," yet each look, act, and tone of his
is as familiar as though he had died but yesterday.
And there are times when an intense longing comes to
me for a "touch of the vanished hand," or a glance
from the heavenly eye.

My friend's bereavement had occurred more re-
cently. Only two years had passed since little Lois
died. She was an only daughter, about eight years of
age, yet thoughtful, almost womanly in her ways.

She was the idol of parents and grand-parents, and
during the long months in which she suffered from dis-

ease her room became the receptacle of many and
choice gifts, brought to cheer her otherwise lonely
hours. Not far from her own little couch were her
dollies, suitably provided with dainty sets of furniture,
and various appointments for housekeeping, over which
Lois presided with a grave and quiet dignity. The
walls of her room were hung with pictures and pretty
trifles, arranged in artistic fashion.

Upon her table were the books and Sunday-school
papers she loved to read, from which, with rare judgment, she would select the best things. Many treasures,
besides, saved up during her short life, which held each
some pleasant memory, or helped her to forget the pain
and weariness, were strewed about. Here and there
were bouquets of grasses, and everlastings, Autumn
leaves, and festoons of vine; and amid these pleasant
surroundings the little sufferer was nearly always happy.

And so she lingered on, tenderly loved and minis-
tered unto, and so patient she was, that friends could
truly say of her, "Of such is the kingdom of heaven."
But at last she grew so weary, that, with a loving kiss
for the dear parents, a tender glance at each of her
treasures, she closed her eyes, to open them upon

brighter scenes and more enduring possessions. More than two years had passed, and the key was turned, that strangers might not look upon the room where Lois died.

To-day it was unlocked, and we, who loved her memory, were permitted to pass the threshold. All was unchanged. Just as her last glance rested upon each possession we found it to day. Each article seemed sacred, for they belonged to Lois now as much as in the days when their presence soothed her pain, and made endurable her weary hours of waiting.

As the sun glanced through the windows, touching in a subdued way the dainty things that Lois loved, we felt that the room, with its surroundings, had been to her almost like the "Mount of Transfiguration," for as one by one the loves of life drifted away, the brighter glories of the world of light unfolded to her view, ample and more than satisfying compensation for all earthly loss.

> Eight years on earth, swift passing years,
> Fraught with life's changes, smiles, and tears;
> Two years since Lois went to rest,
> Two years in Heaven among the blest.

The Earnest Pastor and His Faithful Wife.

I KNOW a faithful wife,
Who gladly gave her youth and beauty,
Her talents, one and all, to God,
And to his service.
To-day she stands beside the man
Who chose her out from all
The worthy multitude,
To aid him in the work of winning souls of men
From sinful ways to pleasant paths.
He, a noble Christian pastor,
Breaking with clean hands the "Bread of Life,"
Touching, with unsullied lips,
The living waters,
Which he gladly offers to other thirsty ones,
That they may drink and live ;—
His aid, God's Spirit and his precious Word.
Among its treasures he finds milk for babes,
And stronger food for older ones,
And by it he is taught
To give to each his portion in its proper time.

Rare and rich in flavor
Is the food he ofttimes serves,
As marrow and as fatness to the hungry soul.
And so as lapsing time marks days and years,
They walk together o'er the chosen way.
Sometimes his strong, brave heart
Seems to grow faint
As heavy burdens press him down,
And then the voice beside him
Quotes sweet, helpful promises,
"Lo I am with you alway, even to the end;"
Be not dismayed, I am thy God.
Or if, perchance,
The clouds above grow thick and dense,
And seem to shut away the lights
That God has hung above them,
Her quick eye sees the little rift
That lets a ray of brightness through;
And then he knows the sun still shines,
And that God's love is over all.
They journey on, and pass, perhaps,
A group of little ones
Who, in the sunrise of their days,

Flit like the butterflies from flower to flower,
And as they gather sweets, leave little
    Benedictions by the way.
And while the pastor and his gentle wife
        Talk to them of the precious Christ,
        Of how he blessed the little ones,
And said, "Of such heaven's kingdom is;"
        Tell how he gave his life
That they might have the best and choicest gift,
        They each resolve to seek and find,
And turn their tender feet the heavenward way,
            Singing, meanwhile,
        Their little songs of peace and love.

        Again they pass a weary pilgrim,
        Bending low above his staff;
        His hands are almost palsied,
And his trembling feet will soon refuse
    To press the sod o'er which he passes
    Toward "the prize beyond the race."
        And as the kindly hands
        Meet his in love and sympathy,
And uttered words like these fall on his ear,

''The mercy of the Lord, to those who keep his Word,
       Forever will endure,''
         His being thrills with joy,
         A foretaste of the rapture unexpressed
           He soon will share.
         Now and then these travelers halt
At pleasant little bowers along the way,
         Where orange blossoms
         Bless the air with fragrance,
And wine of love surcharges youthful hearts
         With hope and happiness;
Where vows and blessings, tears and smiles commingle.
And both the pastor and his wife rejoice and smile,
         And, with a quiet prayer for future weal,
           Go on their way.
Ofttimes they reach the homes
         Where sickness, death,
And bitter mourning sit enthroned.
         And there they tarry longest;
         Where the shadows lengthen, and with
         Harmonious voice, and lip, and touch,
           Chant hymns above the dead,
         Or soothe the souls just going out of life,
         Asking for holy oil for bruised hearts

The while, they tell of rest for His beloved.
And still they journey,
Each watching for the nets and pitfalls
Spread to ensnare their feet,
Each with the shield of prayer and faith
To foil the foe that lurks along the path ;
And if the lions grouped beyond
Seem fierce and terrible, they falter not,
But march with firm and steady step,
To find them chained and powerless ;
For just above are angels,
Who keep watch and ward,
That dangers hedge not up their way.

And thus their lives are crowned with blessings,
And precious memories come drifting in
Of garnered souls,
Which shall be jewels at the last,
Of numbers who have gone before
To welcome them.
Of others who will follow to the blissful shore,
Whom they will meet and welcome,
Saying, as they lead them to the throne,
'' Here am I, Lord, with those thou gavest me.''

Letter from the Queen of Sheba.

[This paper is supposed to have been copied from a parchment nearly three thousand years old, describing the journey of the queen of Sheba from her home in Southern Arabia to Jerusalem, and her reception at the court of Solomon. It was written to the noble "Ahia," scribe and historian to the queen of Sheba, dated month "Nisan," since the days of Adam about three thousand years.]

Chapter I.

AS I have promised to send you tidings of our welfare by each returning caravan, and as we, to-day, have pitched our tents for a few hours at this first oasis we have reached in the desert, refreshing ourselves and camels at the cooling waters, I find refuge from the scorching rays of the sun beneath the broad palms.

My faithful "Cusha" appears with the reed, parchment, and ink horn, desiring to record the events of our journey thus far. Our undertaking was, indeed, formidable. No woman has made so vast a journey since the days that Ham, the son of Noah, settled in this, the uttermost part of the earth. If our ancestors, Cush and Teba, were still living they would look with wonder at one of their own nation with a magnificent

train of camels, laden with choice gifts on her way to
the far north, to visit the greatest king the world has
ever known. According to reports that have reached
our ears the glory and wisdom of Solomon have never
been surpassed. Not even the Pharaohs, with all their
boasted learning and the grandeur of their Egyptian
courts, could compete with the world-renowned Solomon. After bidding you adieu we started in a north-
erly direction, following the old caravan road, keeping
the mountains along the coast in view, catching now
and then from openings in the chain glimpses of the
waters of the Red Sea—so appropriately named from
the red coral found in abundance along its shores.
Away to the right, as far as the eye can reach, are
sandy plains with only now and then a few palms and an
occasional spring to relieve the monotony of the desert.

My fleet-footed camel moves proudly over the sands
as if conscious of her errand, and the saddle embroid-
ered by your direction is the admiration of all our
company. The pack camels are laden with every
needful comfort, and travelers say our outfit is the
most perfect they have seen.

For ten days we have traveled, and no calamity has

overtaken us.   We passed, yesterday, a mountain of
sand, the effects of one of the terrible winds that sweep
across the desert, which turned us for some distance
from the route of travel.   We dismounted, prostrating
ourselves in token of gratitude that the "simoon" had
not made us graves in the desert.   Our guide, who
was one of the skilled workmen sent by Hiram, king
of Tyre, to aid Solomon in building the "Temple,"
not only leads us by the safest routes, but continually
interests us by accounts of Solomon and his wealth
and power.   He has also had access to the history of
their nation, and I am more deeply impressed each
day as I hear of God's miraculous dealings with them,
that he is the same God who furnished in a wonderful
manner the lamb to our father Abraham when about
to sacrifice his only son, and that he will become the
God of the whole earth.   I will say to you my friend
and counselor what our people do not know, that my
heart cries out for something more satisfactory than
our vague ideas of God, and although I desire to see
Solomon, and hear his words of wisdom, yet I hope to
find a greater than Solomon ere I return to my southern home.

Chapter II.

WE passed, this morning, so near the harbor, south of the eastern arm of the sea, that we had a fine view of one of the ships belonging to the navy built by Solomon.

Our guide Amaziah, the Tyrian, left us a little while to day, asking the loan of two camels, one to be saddled for use, the other carrying an empty pack-saddle. He promised to be back at the noonday hour. In the mean time we feast our eyes upon Sinai, whose rugged heights are plainly discerned across the gulf, which is perhaps six or eight miles in width at this point. On leaving, our guide placed in my hands a scroll, which contains an account of the ascent of Moses, the law-giver, to Sinai's summit, where for twice forty days he dwelt with God. It was here that the tables of stone were prepared, and the law written by the finger of God, and from the parchment I learn that the same tables of stone were deposited in an ark prepared for them, taken to the land of the Israelites, and are now in the Temple at Jerusalem.

Can it be possible that my eyes will ever behold the

handwriting of God; will my ears be gladdened by the sound of words from his lips? Our good Amaziah is coming, but not alone. I must hasten to be arrayed in purple to receive a guest. My maidens tell me it is the daughter of the king of Tyre,* Armaiah by name, and that she has been for some months a dweller in the house of Solomon's wife. This accounts for her Egyptian costume, as the queen still clings to the customs of the land of her birth. The vessel, it appears, has been waiting some days for our caravan, and this youthful princess, through an arrangement of Solomon, is to be my companion. I can not receive her as in my beautiful palace at home, but must hasten to her with words of greeting.

Chapter III.

I FIND the princess exceedingly lovely; her fair fresh beauty is of the northern type, for her childhood was passed where the breezes from Lebanon fanned her brow, and she could bathe in waters from the snows of Hermon. She has just been telling me that thirty thousand men were sent to the mountains to prepare

---

*Tradition gathered from Commentary.

timber to be used in the Temple, and of the fir trees and cedar trees, that were brought in floats from Tyre to Joppa, thence conveyed by ox-carts overland to Jerusalem.

She has a profound admiration for Solomon, but is in love with the queen, and has not only adopted the costume of the Egyptian ladies, but is learning their forms of worship. Among her treasures are idols brought from the banks of the Nile, and she tells me that the Egyptian maidens who serve the queen all worship idols. My heart yearns over the young girl, and I hope we may both find our way to the true God.

We find many points of interest as we hasten onward, for we often cross the old trail of the Israelites, who through disobedience, it is said, wandered for years in the wilderness. I find by the record that their food was rained down from heaven, and their thirst assuaged from the smitten rock; that the pillar of cloud that went before them by day, and of fire by night, denoted God's constant presence; and yet they distrusted him, and joined themselves to their idols.

5

Chapter IV.

WE miss the bracing atmosphere as we get farther
from the sandy plains, but we find more abundant vegetation, wells more frequent, and groves numerous; and
here· we pitch our tents, that the camels may rest after
their wearisome march.   We find the princess, Armaiah, quite learned.   She has met with ambassadors
from many nations of the earth, and has gathered from
the scribes in the king's household knowledge of their
customs, and of the lands in which they dwell.   She has
just been describing her visit, as companion of Solomon's wife, to Tadmor, called by the Greeks Palmyra.
The city is built in the heart of the Syrian Desert, and
is a proud monument of Solomon's glory.

No city in the world equals it in magnificence.
Even Jerusalem, the dwelling place of the king, can
not compare with Tadmor in the desert.   Here the
caravans between the Mediterranean and the Euphrates
meet and interchange commodities through this chan-
nel.   The East and the West pour their wealth into the
coffers of Solomon, and with unsparing hand has he
lavished it upon tower and column, altar and temple,

until this great mart of commerce has become the wonder of the world.

We are now traveling rapidly toward the borders of the land of Canaan, and although I had hoped to pass along the eastern shore of the Dead Sea, visit Mount Nebo, from whose summit Israel's lawgiver saw the "Promised Land," journey through Moab, where God buried Moses, and cross the Jordan just where the Ark was borne over by the priests, yet our guide tells me the shortest way is through the Wilderness of Judah; and as my errand is urgent, we hasten by the nearest route. To-night we encamp near Hebron, where is the cave of Machpelah, bought by Abraham for a burial place.

Here he was buried with Sarah, his wife; also Leah, Isaac, and Rebecca were here entombed, and Jacob, who died in Egypt. How strange that I may look upon the tomb of my ancestors, some of whom were buried five hundred years ago. Another day and we shall encamp under the shadow of Mount Moriah. Amaziah, the Tyrian, has already sent a message to the court of Solomon of our near approach. The thought that I am about to visit "The Temple," God's accepted dwelling place, seems to leave no spirit in me. That his presence overshadows it I am sure, for it is said when the tables of stone were placed within the Holy of Holies a cloud of glory filled the house.

The messengers have returned with tidings that a portion of the house of the forest of Lebanon is set apart for our use, and that my men and camels will be taken in charge by the governor of the king's household. Amaziah, who is skilled in works of art, will arrange the gifts we have brought, and Armaiah, whom I have learned to love, will go with me to the presence of Solomon.

Chapter V.

THE day so long looked for has come and gone. We have had audience with the wisest king of earth. We are told that God bade Solomon ask what he most desired, and he asked wisdom. Truly it has been given him in large measure.

He received us in the porch of the house of Lebanon, which is fifty cubits in length. The camels were unladen, and the gifts arranged according to their value. The precious stones, the ivory, the gold and silver,

Solomon's Temple.

tortoise shell from the rock Perim, myrrh, and spices, with the choice balsam that only grows in our country.

The king rejoiced at sight of the royal gifts, and gave orders that on our return the camels be reladen with fragrant woods from the forest of Lebanon, elegant embroideries, and rare commodities from Palmyra, to which the wife of Solomon will add choice specimens of Egyptian workmanship.

Chapter VI.

BUT all these things are of small account compared to the knowledge I have gained of our fathers' God. Abraham, Isaac, and Jacob trusted in him; he was in the wilderness forty years with Moses and Joshua; he talked with David and gave Solomon his heart's desire; henceforth, he is to be my guide and the helper of my people.

The glory of Solomon's kingdom I can not describe. The house of Lebanon, the king's house, and the palace of the queen, with their furnishings, to which the whole earth has contributed its rare and costly products, makes me feel the half has not been told. But the Temple is the crowning glory of Solomon's work.

Hither I am drawn each day to worship, and as I commune with the king of all that is in my heart, or study the law given by God through Moses, a light like the glory that filled the Temple seems to illumine my understanding and dissolve my doubts.

I am learning that the sacrifices are but types of the purer offering suggested by the words of Moses and the patriarchs; and as I look upon the veil which hides from view the Holy of Holies I know it will some time be lifted and the "glory that was with the Father before the world was" shall be revealed.

The Temple built without the sound of hammer, with its perfect architecture, its beautiful proportions, its ornaments of gold and precious stones, is a prophecy of a house not made with hands held in reserve for God's obedient children; and as by the wisdom of Solomon I have been taught these precious truths, I am led to say "Blessed be the Lord thy God which delighted in thee, to set thee on the throne of Israel, because the Lord loved Israel forever; therefore. made he the king to do judgment and justice."

An Hour with a Picture.

THE day was long and lonely, for the cheery group that brightened my home had flitted out for a time, and the rooms were desolate.

So to comfort myself I picked up a roll of pictures, rare engravings and pencilings. As I glanced at each they had a sad or pleasant story to tell. But I lingered longest over a dainty cross, with draping of ivy, all tastefully wrought by fingers that were now stilled. My thoughts went back a few years to the time when the fair young girl whose handiwork it was came to us to pursue her chosen avocation as teacher.

She was a delicate creature, fair to behold, high-souled, and strong of will in the right; and although she had a few trials, she had much success, and many friends.

And so the long Summer days went and came in brightness or cloud, as was their wont, unmindful of the shadows that followed her footsteps. She often spoke of her future as desiring to do some good work for God and humanity, but as she strove to mark out her

way, in one or the other direction, an abrupt angle
would shut the future from view, or unexpected obstacles would arise, until her path seemed lost in the years.

But she laid her hand in the hand of the Father,
and tried to walk as he seemed to lead. After a time
came an urgent request, from a friend in a distant city,
to come to her for the Winter months. So she laid
aside her burden of work and care, and went with a purpose to be happy, and to help make bright the home
where she was to be a welcome and honored guest.

And she did enjoy, with a rare zest, the beautiful
things by which she was surrounded. And the months
seemed all too short for the blessings that crowded
themselves into her life. In the early Spring came pre-
monitions of disease, and friends feared the shadows
that had followed in the distance were gathering
strength; but she fought bravely, and at last rallied,
hoping yet to do some work before she went to the
better country.

She wrote cheering letters, and the light of hope
rested on her brow. Soon again the shadows drifted in
and out, each time tarrying a little longer, until at last
friends knew that death lingered near, and time was

hastening the sad result. Mother and friends were summoned to her side. All was done that love could prompt or gold could buy, but of no avail.

She saw her way clear, at last, up to the very throne where Christ as mediator sat, and understood why one and the other chosen path had been hedged up.

The home and the love toward which she was tending seemed very delightful to her. She prepared calmly to enter upon her untried future, only asking that her remains might be laid in the cemetery she loved, by the friends still dear, and then peacefully died. She had left us bright and hopeful.

When we saw her again she was robed for burial. Loving hands had done their work well and tastefully; and so lovely she looked, it seemed as if the angel of death must sorrow over the work he had wrought.

Above the feet, that would never again grow tired, or be wounded by the roughness of the way, a beautiful mossy mound was fashioned, through which was enwrought, with snowy buds, the word "*Rest.*"

How we rejoiced with and for her, as we looked at this beautiful prophecy of her future, and knew that she was realizing its fulfillment; while to us it was a

harbinger of hope, of the possibilities in store for us.
She had reached at last the "Land of the Leal," where
no more *crosses* were to be builded or borne; where no
dark shadows could interpose to hide the brightness;
"where the nations of them that are saved shall walk
in the light of it, and the kings of the earth shall bring
their glory and honor into it."

One of My Treasures.

AMONG my treasures is a beautiful and costly book.
Its elegant binding, its tinted golden edged leaves,
and rare engravings, all speak to me of the love
which prompted this delicate gift.

Its subject matter thrills my heart, for it tells of my
Christ, his pure life, his sufferings, and sacrifices, while
each page directs me to the "Lamb for sinners slain."
Inclosed is a tiny sheet of paper, upon which I find in
delicate tracery, the names of the Sabbath-school class
which I have tried, for many months, to lead heavenward. Hidden among the leaves of my book are the

faces that I meet from Sabbath to Sabbath. Among
them are good and noble girls, who have early learned to
sit at the Savior's feet and be taught of him. They have
exalted views of life, and its duties, and will go forth
as earnest workers in the "Master's vineyard." Others
there are who have not yet yielded to the claims of the
Gospel, but their lives are so consistent, their innate
nobleness so apparent, that we are justly proud of their
pure record, and feel assured they will soon be gathered
into the fold.

A fair young wife who has known much of sorrow,
is with us, learning to rest in Christ. From early childhood she has so needed a Savior's guiding hand, and
we rejoice that she has found him "the chief among
ten thousand." Perchance *she* is to be made perfect
through suffering. A dear girl from the sunny South
has come to us, half orphaned and struggling with
trials. May the promise, "I will never leave thee nor
forsake thee," be verified to her.

The bright face of a boy of twelve Summers is
among the group. He brings to the class a knowledge
of each subject under consideration far ahead of his
years; but we know he was the only son of an invalid

mother, who by constant and prayerful labors, as she drifted toward the grave, succeeded in implanting in his heart a portion of her own beautiful faith, as well as a saving knowledge of the "way of life." The loving mother grew more and more feeble, and one day in the early springtime she went home. May her prayers and teachings be an enduring legacy to the orphaned son.

The dear circle is now broken ; some of the loved ones, at duty's call, have found other homes ; but I expect to meet them all again, and our trysting place will be among Eden's bowers. When the Master makes up his jewels, may each member of the class be there to receive " The robe and the crown."

Keepsakes.

HAVE a drawer full of gathered treasures,
   Some given in life's morning long since past ;
They tell me of the precious love unmeasured,
   The love that through unending years will last.

I have a book, both old and quaint in fashion ;
   Its leaves once fair, are now by time defaced.

'T was a reward of merit, I remember,
  And on its first blank page two names are traced.

I have a little coin in tarnished silver.
  It tells me of a battle fought mid tears and pain,
And how at last I came away a victor,
  For right had triumphed and its foe was slain.

I have a roll of writing, scraps, and sermons,—
  The hands that wrote were folded long ago ;
I have a fragment of a wedding garment,
  With silken letters woven through and through.

I have a linen cap, by nimble fingers netted,
  Its crown and border wrought in dainty lace ;
And well do I remember how it covered
  The snowy hair, and wreathed the placid face.

I have a picture almost hid in shadows,—
  The loving eyes are dim, only outlined ;
The face is full of sweet and patient sadness,—
  No marvel why, for the dear eyes were blind.

I have a flower, woven from threads of hair,
  A fadeless flower, the fruit of thoughtful love :
It hung, a dainty curl, above a brow most fair,—
  The wearer now dwells in the home above.

I have an apron, worn by tiny maid
    ('T is yellow now, but once 't was white as snow).
She was a winsome, loving little thing,—
    The Savior called and she went long ago.

I have a comb, and it was used to fasten
    The raven tresses of a sister's hair.
She called her children to her side one morning,
    And kissed them all, and died 'mid breath of prayer.

I can not name the half of all my treasures,
    Their value more to me than wealth in gold;
To other eyes they would not seem so precious,
    But each to me some tender memory holds.

More dear than all, the uttered words at parting
    With the dear friends, whose wings were plumed for
        flight;
More precious was the glory shed about them,
    As if reflected from the world of light.

Yet better still will be the words of greeting,
    That we shall hear from lips unstained by sin;
And full of bliss will be the joyful meeting,
    When Christ our Advocate shall bid us enter in.

An Incident of Travel.

RAVELING on the Erie road not long since, I became interested in those who came and went from our own car. As the train halted at an important station, I saw, standing upon the platform, two ladies engaged in pleasant converse, showing by every look, act, and word that they loved each other tenderly. As I observed them more closely, I fancied a resemblance as between mother and daughter, and was quite sure, at last, that the daughter was a resident of the pretty town through which we were journeying. While absorbed in their pleasant companionship the signal for departure was given. The good-byes were hastily spoken, a whispered prayer, I knew, was breathed from each, and they separated. The mother entered the car in which I was seated, while the daughter stood watching, with tear-wet eyes, for the last look and final waving of farewell, as the train passed from her sight. My thoughts lingered with the daughter, glancing back a few short years, perhaps to the time, when a bride, she had gone out from her childhood's home, loving the husband who had chosen her and well beloved by him, and yet I knew an aching void was left that the new home and pleasant surroundings, even the love of her heart's chosen, could not fill. For *often* she must yearn for a sight of the home faces, and for the tender parental care that sheltered her in childhood.

A movement of the mother recalled me from my reverie, and, as she lifted her bowed head, I knew she too had been thinking of the "dear eldest born;" of their homes so far separated; of the time that must intervene ere they might meet again; of the possibility that sickness or death might make the separation final; and, as my eye met hers, the mother-love revealed itself so strongly, that my heart was drawn instinctively toward her. Rising, I took from a niche, in the side of the car, a Bible, placed there by divine inspiration (I am sure), and laid it in her hand. She gave me a quick, grateful look, and turning the leaves read lesson after lesson from its pages, marking here and there; and as I watched her she seemed to grow comforted. Later I lifted the volume to find the words which had soothed her heart, and read this text: "Like as a father pitieth his children, so the Lord pitieth them that fear him." And another: "The mercy of the Lord is from everlasting to everlasting upon them that fear him, and his righteousness unto children's children, to such as keep his covenant, and to those that remember his commandments to do them."

And I rejoiced at the fullness of the Gospel, that in every sorrow or emergency that might come into our lives some comforting word or helpful promise is given.

God Magnified in His Works.

PSALM VIII.

WHEN I consider thy heavens, unrolled like a scroll,
 A marvel of vastness, of majesty sublime,
 Eternal in breadth, like duration of soul,
  Created far back in the youthhood of time;

When I remember the great plan was made,
In thy secret chambers the corners were laid,
That thou, the Creator, with marvelous skill,
Thine own hands with beauty the heavens did fill
6

From thy hidden treasures, thy storehouse of light,
The moon and the stars, thy gifts to the night,
In thine own pavilion thy thought did ordain,
And their voices thy greatness and glory proclaim—

We can but inquire, O what is man,
Thou art mindful of him in thy wondrous plan—
Man, humble, and lowly, and full of sin,
And yet thou deignest to visit him?

But in thy precious Word thou hast said
That man little lower than angels was made,
That dominion and power to him should be given,
Honor on earth and a crown in heaven.

Our Pastor.

THERE came to us to minister in holy things,
    A man chosen from out the common herd;
    His heart was filled with love of souls,
And all his wealth of intellect was called to aid
        In winning them to Christ.
        Earnest and faithful,

He labored as those who give account;
And for his hire the hearts of men
      Were turned to God.
More precious far to him such pay
      Than gold or precious stones.
Such an one God delights to honor,
      While the good and wise
      Render to him the homage due to one
      Stamped with the impress of his Maker.

And those who did not love the truths he preached,
While listening to his burning words,
      Were well assured
That he was one of God's anointed. . . .

Our Savior chastens whom he loves,
    And so our friend and pastor felt
That pain and anguish came by his permissive providence.
    He loved his Christian calling,
    And labored on through failing strength
Until his poor, worn frame refused to bear him
    To the temple of the Lord.
    And then his mourning flock came to his side—
The gray-haired men, who like the Aarons and the Hurs,

Had held his hands from falling;
And the dear mothers of the Church,
Who loved their pastor, and were by him beloved;
Young men and maidens,
Who, through him, were taught the better way;
And little children, whose fair brows
His hand and voice had blessed, all came,
With hopeful words and loving gifts,
And bade him rest and seek for strength,
That later he might come to them again.
And yet they sorrowed, as did the elders,
When they bade farewell to Paul,
Fearing that they might see his face no more.
'Twas then the burden of men's souls
Was lifted from him for a time,
And in its place a longing came
For health restored,
Hoping with added power and life renewed
To do grand work in years to come.
And though his constant heritage was pain,
He roused himself,
To seek the needful help mid other scenes.
Hither and thither, like dove of old,

He wandered, seeking rest,
            Drinking of crystal fountains,
As he prayed that they might be to him
            As living waters,
Taking from skilled hands the balm,
That we all hoped might give a lease of added years.
        And yet he thought of God, and heaven,
            His future home, with rare delight,
And fed his faith with precious promises,
            Praying each day the prayer,
        "Thy will, not mine, be done."
            And while we watched and waited
            The result with anxious hearts,
We seem to hear the words prophetic,
        "It is enough, come higher up."
Infinite goodness made the struggle short,
For while loved ones still clung to him,
            With grasp persistent,
The pearly gates were opened, and he looked within the
        veil.
The glories of the inner temple were revealed,
While voice, far sweeter than the notes of angels,
Breathed in his ear, "Ye blessed of my Father, come

Take thine inheritance prepared so long ago."
 A backward look, words full of tenderness
  To mourning friends,
 And then with song of praise upon his lips,
  His eyes were closed to earth.
 And thus our pastor entered into rest.

———⧫———

The Lily and the Rose.

FROM THE GERMAN FABLE BY HERDER.

FAIR daughters of the rough black earth,
  Tell me, wilt ye,
 Who gave your beautiful forms?
 Skilled fingers, surely, fashioned you.
What spirits mounted up your tiny cups?
  And were you pleased
To see them rocking on your leaves?
 Say to me, silent flowers,
How did they share among themselves
  Their joyous task?
And did they beckon to each other,
 As they spun so skillfully,

Or made embroideries to adorn your texture delicate?
  Lovely children, you are silent,
  And well enjoy your life.
    The learned fable shall relate
What your lips are unwilling to reveal.

    The earth once stood, a naked rock,
When, lo! a friendly multitude of nymphs
  Brought virgin soil to spread it o'er;
  And spirits kind, were ready soon
To deck with flowers the naked rock.
    In various ways they shared their task;
Already, 'neath the snow, in the small grass,
  Modest humility, in secret wore,
The self-concealing violet.
    Hope came close after,
Filling with cooling fragrance
    The refreshing hyacinth.
Now, since these had well succeeded, came a haughty
    throng
Of beauties, many hued. The tulip raised its head,
The pale narcissus glanced about with longing eye,
And many nymphs and goddesses were busied now,
In various ways, adorning earth,

Rejoicing in their beauteous work.
But, lo! when time had passed,
A greater portion of their work had faded;
Its glory paled,
And their delight in it was gone.

Then Venus thus addressed the graces, three:
Why tarry, sisters fair, of gracefulness?
Why are ye idle?
Take of your charms, arise and weave
A blossom mortal, visible.
They went to earth, and one Aglaia,
The grace of innocence, fashioned the lily fair,
Then Thalia and her sister wrought the flower
Of joy and love, the virgin rose.
Many flowers of field and garden
Have envy each to other;
The lily and the rose unenvious,
Are envied of them all.
As sisters they bloom together,
On their plot of Spring,
And each doth grace the other,
Their lives conjointly woven,
In grace of sisterhood.

The Old Door-Yard.

The Old Door Yard.

THE dear old yard, with its tangled green;
   Its great long beds, with the walks between;
   The lilacs tall, reaching up to the eaves,
With their fragrant bloom, and their wealth of leaves.

How fresh it all looks since the early storm,
That came in such earnest, this very morn,
As if mother nature, most surely did mean,
That grasses and flowers should all be kept clean.

And well they enjoyed the bath, I am sure;
Their faces look fresh, and their garments are pure;
And they lift up their heads, as if they would say,
We have on our company robes to-day.

And the peony says to the dainty bluebell,
I am sure, little dear, that you look very well,
But for my part, I like gorgeous colors to wear,
Of my beauty, you surely must be well aware.

And the bluebells, and whitebells, smiled each in its way,
And asked of the other, what ought they to say,

For they cared very little for colors or show,
They only desired their duty to know.

They finally thought to say nothing at all,
For soon it would fade, and its "pride take a fall;"
And so they just bowed their wise little heads,
'T will the sooner be mended, if little is said.

And the roses laughed, as the breezes came,
And touched their bloom with colors aflame,
Or draped them in robes of dainty white,
Or in warmer glow, like the sunset's light.

And the rose, that looked most like the sea-shell's heart,
Was honored the most, and set apart,
To place at the throat, or in braids of hair,
Of the maiden beloved, so wondrously fair,

Who wandered about, 'mid the grasses and flowers,
Or hid herself deep in the green old bowers,
To listen to what the roses would say,
As they whispered, and nodded, and threw sweets away.

The fragrant syringa looked on in its pride.
Its pure creamy blossoms are fit for a bride,
While its sheltering arms give comfort and shade,
To the tiny home the yellow birds made.

The little white lilies resolved not to stay;
In the bed they were planted, but wandered away,
To hide themselves down in the grasses alone,
As the bride and her husband seek out a new home.

Honeysuckles climb at their own sweet will,
As if gathering nectar, their cups to fill;
And the song-birds hasten their way to wing,
'Mid its tangled sweetness, their songs to sing.

And stately great lilies, with coats of old gold,
Are marshaled in groups, as if converse to hold;
While the dark velvet pansies nestle down at their feet,
For purple and gold, royal colors, should meet.

Close by the old well, the cherry tree stands,
Where the grey squirrels meet, to talk of their plans,
And wonder if down in the trunk they could store
More food than they placed there the Autumn before.

Evergreens stand by the door yard gate.
With their boughs entwined, they patiently wait,
And watch o'er the growth of each bud and each flower,
Rejoicing at sunshine, and glad of the shower.

Choice fruit trees are scattered here and there,
And they teach us a lesson of faith and prayer;

For God has revealed, by unfailing sign,
That fruitage shall come, in his own good time.

The wayside maples lift high up their heads,
Though smiling down still at the flower beds,
And the sun rays are glinting the boughs between,
Making golden mosaic, on emerald green.

Thus the Father's great love, in his works is displayed,
For the earth in its fullness, for us he has made;
His beautiful gifts are to all freely given,
Till earth's needs are met by the beauties of heaven.

The Double Funeral.

THE bell was tolling,
   Its measured voice reached up and down the
       village streets,
Telling the funeral hour had come.
The town was all astir, as from each home
The inmates came to look upon the faces of the dead.
     The crowd came surging in,
Filling the church, all save the mourners' seats,

Until the aisles were packed, galleries were crowded,
And sympathizing friends were grouped without,
With reverent hearts, as the two coffined forms,
Were borne within the portals, and placed side by side.

Then came the father, bent with age and sorrow.
  By his side the widow of his son,
Who, stricken down in manhood's prime,
   Had died three days ago.
Next, with trembling feet, the mother followed,
  Led by the husband of her eldest born,
   A daughter idolized in life,
Who passed away in early morn of yesterday,
Brothers and sisters of the dead bearing a double weight
  of woe.
    And children,
  Who had never known a grief
  Until this bitter hour,
  Were seated round their dead.

   A tide of sorrow
  Seemed to sweep o'er every heart,
For we had known and loved the brother and the sister
  in their early years;

Had watched the young girl's budding womanhood,
Rejoiced with her when one, who seemed well worthy,
  won her to his side,
And bore her to his sunny home in other lands;
Had heard, with thankful hearts, of fortune's smile,
And sorrowed, when the mournful tidings came,
  Of her heart's idol shattered,
Of broken health, of fevered cheek, and racking cough,
And how she wanted to come home to die.

A few days later the manly brother,
Who still tarried in his early home,
On whose strong arm the aged parents hoped to lean
As they went down the western slope of life,
Went forth to meet the sister, who had journeyed far
  To look again upon the dear, home group.
How he wept at sight of the white face and wasted hands,
As tenderly he bore her to the couch
Where she had slept and dreamed in childhood's hour;
Where breath of honeysuckle drifted in,
And climbing roses bowed their heads in grief
  At sight of the poor wasted form
  They fain would heal and bless.

The weeks went slowly by,
As the poor sufferer languished on her bed of pain,
Happier when the brother,
By whose side she sported in the olden time,
Could sit beside to soothe the aching head,
Or wet the fevered lips.
And mother's touch was not more tender,
Or mother's love more thoughtful;
It almost seemed as if the angels must have helped,
So quiet were his footsteps,
So comforting each word he uttered, so restful his
caress,
That even death seemed loath to sever hearts thus joined,
And waited for a little time.

A lovely morning dawned:
The sister knew the weary watcher needed change,
A breath of purer air,
And bade him go, adown the vale, and gather mint,
And bring some wildwood flowers,
Wet with the early dew.
He, thinking
To tempt her dainty appetite, shouldered his gun,

Hoping to bring a bird or squirrel
　　　From the woodland depths.
Meanwhile she slept a long and restful sleep, and woke
　　refreshed,
But missed her faithful nurse; yet smiled to think
He might have found some quiet nook,
　　　And, soothed by nature's lullaby,
Was sleeping too, as she had seen him sleep,
　　　When wearied in boyhood's days.
And her heart grew warm
With memories of his tenderness in those old days;
And then she thought of all his weary watching,
In these later hours of pain,
And her spirit joyed for such a royal gift,
　　　A brother's love.

　　The sun climbed higher,
　　And the day had numbered half its hours,
　　And still he lingered.
　　The noonday meal was spread,
But none could taste until the truant came;
And so one went to find and bring him home.
　　No answering shout returned the call,

But, following on his track
By the bruised flowers his feet had pressed,
Too soon they came upon his shattered form ;
    A broken arm, a wounded side,
    From which the blood oozed forth,
    Told all too plain the awful truth,—
    The noble, manly heart had ceased to beat.

Tongue can not tell, nor pen portray
The darkness that o'erspread that home,
    Expressed in such a cry
As rose throughout the land of Egypt,
    When one lay dead in every house.
    The sister only gave no sign,
But folded her thin hands, and prayed to die,
    And to be buried by his side,
As if the grave would be less dark if he were near.

Quiet forms moved softly through the shadowed rooms,
    And tender hands arrayed the dead.
Sweet promises were spoken to the stricken one,
Who faded hour by hour, until in early dawn
The watchers saw the white lips move,
    And, bending low,

7

Caught whispered words:
"I go to him, he shall no more return to me;"
And then, and thus her prayer was answered.

The aged pastor rose from out his place
And, with a simple, trusting faith,
Asked God to bind anew the broken hearts,
And sanctify to all the sad bereavement of the hour.
While he read an old, familiar hymn,
He spoke of those who, not long since
Had joined with them in praise,
As listening now to songs of the redeemed.
His text, "Lovely in life, in death divided not,"
Might have been written for the time and place.

A backward look o'er three decades
Brought to the pastor's mind
Two children, full of life and beauty,
Tripping through tangled forest maze,
Or playing in the shadow of the orchard trees,
Or, hand in hand,
With dinner basket on their way to school.
And thus the sunny hours of childhood,
As free from care as drifting cloud, went by.

Later they grew more thoughtful,
As God revealed his will,
The sacrifice of Christ the son,
  Their duty to obey the call,
" My son, my daughter, give to me thine heart."
  They tarried not, but gladly yielded,
    Giving youth, and time, and talents,
      Hoping thus to honor God.
And then their lives took on new beauties,
As they went forth among the poor, afflicted ones of
    earth,
  With needed gifts and cheery words,
Until their names were almost held in reverence
In the lowly homes they strove to brighten.

  Still another memory was recalled,
    Of how a joyous multitude
    Had wandered out from the old home
      One bright Spring day ;
And some were clad in snowy robes and flowing veils,
    with tiny lilies wreathed,
And, under the old oaks, marriage vows were spoken.
  And thus the brother and the sister

Left their childhood and their youth behind,
And entered on the untried path ;
While faith and hope, attendant angels, spoke of pleas-
    ant shades,
And cooling streams, and quiet resting places all along
    the way.

      Or if, perchance, the shadows
    Might sometimes cross their path,
And the sweet waters be made bitter to the taste,
And storms should come to them, instead of brightness,
They would be strong, for each would help the other
    Until the path was trodden o'er,
And they should rest together at the last.
      Brief were the old man's words,
    Until he reached the final clause,
        " In death divided not."
Then he aroused himself,
    As though he too stood by the valley ;
    Saw the shadows lift themselves,
    Looked o'er the narrow stream,
And glanced within the gates that stood ajar,
Seeming to see the forms that now we mourned.

He told with burning words, how through eternal years
These united hearts would hold sweet converse,
As the glories which were shadowed to them now
  Would be revealed in fuller depths,
  As added years of immortality·
Should bring to them a clearer vision
And more perfect knowledge of God's wondrous plans.

We laid them down, beneath the spreading oaks,
Where they had stood one bright day in the past,
  Surrounded by the friends they loved the best.
To-day the same dear forms were found above their
  grave.
  Smiles were replaced by tears;
Instead of bridal robes were mourning garbs;
In place of whispered prophecies
  Of long and happy years on earth,
We heard of life eternal, and the fairer land.
  A broad white marble slab
  Is placed above them.
And the passer-by may read the chiseled words,
  "Lovely in life, in death divided not."

Lines to a Daffodil.

DAFFODIL, thou bright Spring flower,
 Blooming under cold gray skies,
  It almost seems as if the raw Spring winds
Would drive thee back to thy warm Winter's nest,
 Where last year's sunbeams found thee;
And in the long cold Winter days,
Wrought wondrous changes in thy homely bulb,
 And sent thee forth in gorgeous dress,
A prophecy of sunny skies, and balmy air,
 And troops of other flowers that charm as well,
 But lack thy courage, yellow daffodil.

Longings for Home.

IT was midnight of Friday, and we were to wait two
long hours — a weary waiting for tired travelers.
There was a good deal of uneasiness among them,
for two or three parties were to sail if they could make

the connection by one or another of the lines of Saturday steamers.

Among them an old man, who must have reached his threescore years and ten, was especially restless. He walked with slow and trembling steps back and forth, leaning upon his staff, inquiring now and then the time of night, how soon the train would be due, and would they reach their destination in season. A young man, his traveling companion, evidently a relative, answered his questions, kindly trying to reassure him.

From him we learned that the aged man was homesick. Many years before he had left his father's cottage on the banks of the river Trent, in the north of England, and coming to America had found a home in a distant State. He had been abundantly prospered, had sons and daughters settled near, but since the death of his wife a spirit of unrest had come upon him, a longing that would not be put down, to see the home of his youth. He talked of it by day and dreamed of it by night, and at last resolved to make the journey; to look again upon his native fields, the orchards, and the river, the graves of his parents, and the dear old

roof under which he slept in childhood, thinking to return in peace to his children, to die, and be buried in
the land of his adoption. It hardly seemed as if his
hopes would be realized—so feeble he was—but should
his life be spared to look upon the old familiar scenes
he might be satisfied to go from there to the better
land, where age and weariness are unknown, where in
the enjoyment of perpetual youth he might dwell with
the dear kindred from beyond the broad ocean, who
would finally be gathered with those who slumbered in
the old burial places, in final and happy reunion.

Another face interested me, the face of a pale tired-
looking woman, who seemed absorbed in the care of
her two young daughters.

She had a hungry, yearning look, as if something
was lost out of her life. She was dressed plainly,
almost shabbily, and the garments of her children
showed rigid economy.

Through a little attention to the children I succeeded in winning the confidence of the mother. She
told me of the long voyage she was to take back to
the "dear father-land;" of the home she had left beyond the Mississippi; how she had gone there with her

husband in the morning of their married life with hopes
of acquiring a competence; how through all the years
her husband had toiled hopefully, amid sickness and
reverses and manifold discouragements; how at the last
her health was broken, and of her longing for a sight
of the dear old father and mother, until it seemed as
if she would die if her wish was denied. She told me
further that the scanty purse would not permit them
all to go, and that the unselfish husband had stayed to
take care of their little home. She tried to describe
her parents as they looked twelve years ago when she
left them, and the quaint little house, their home, and
the stream, and the mill, and the little church, until it
seemed to me like an old memory revived.

As we again took our places in the car, and sped
toward the great ocean, my thoughts followed the
brave little woman through her long journey, saw the
greeting from the dear friends who received her almost
as from the dead, realized how strength must come
back to her slight form through the tender ministry of
a "mother's love;" and I thought, too, of the time, a
few months hence, when she would return to her patient, self-sacrificing husband, with added love, born of

his tender care for her, with the health and beauty of her girlhood restored, and my heart was lifted to the home of the finally faithful, where every longing will be satisfied, "and God shall wipe away all tears from their eyes, and there shall be no more death, neither sorrow, nor crying, neither shall there be any more pain, for the former things are passed away."

My Father's Bible.

A BOOK I have, well worn and soiled, 'tis true,
  But dearer far to me
Than massive libraries of earthly love,
 For it is hallowed by the touch
Of fingers long since crumbled into dust.
  Doubly precious are its truths,
As I remember that the eyes that smiled in mine,
  In childhood days,
Have scanned its pages o'er and o'er.
  The story fresh to-day as when first penned.
About creation's morn, the birth of centuries,

The wondrous work wrought by God's hand,
  When first from chaos earth was made,
  And clothed with grace and beauty,
While its heart was stored with treasures
  That would bless all future time.
      It tells, besides,
  How God made day and night,
  And of the lights he placed on high,
    Ordained in such grand fashion,
That as we try to comprehend their vastness,
And find the sources of the light and heat,
    We lose ourselves as truly
As if we tried by power of thought
To fathom the unmeasured life of God.
    In this old book we also read
That man was formed in God's own image,
And placed in Eden bowers,
      And to him given
All beautiful and pleasant things,
Save one, the tree of which God said,
"If thou dost eat, most surely thou shalt die."
    But poor, weak man,
Forgetful of the god-like gift implanted in his heart,

Yielded to baser thought,
And ate of the forbidden fruit,
And in disgrace was driven forth to labor and to death.
We read that ages came and went,
And nations multiplied,
And sin stalked o'er the earth,
While death came with its blight to every home;
And how God's heart at last was softened
Toward his creatures,
And that with helpful plan he came to earth,
And in the mount, whose brow was hidden in the
cloud,
Made his abode, and framed his laws,
And through his chosen servant
Gave them to a gathered multitude,
Who, if obedient, should have his help and aid
To find the rest they sought.
Again we turn the leaves of this old book,
And read of one, a youthful shepherd,
Who communed with God, as with a friend,
Studying the mystery of the sky o'erhead, his roof by
day and night,
As he went forth o'er the green earth.

Leading his flocks from sunny pastures on the mountain
  side,
To grassy vales and cooling streams beneath,
And then again to loftier heights, chanting in noble
  strains
  Of him who made his chariot of a cloud.
  O, how his lofty words comfort our hearts;
For we may know that if we live as David did
Upon the mountain top, we, too, shall hear the words
  of God,
  And gladly lift our voices in his praise.
    Later, the prophets came;
A half a score or more, like sons of Anak in strength
  and power,
Yet with cleared vision, and stronger mental grasp,
Which gave such knowledge of the good in store
  That made it seem as if they shared
  The sweet counsels of the Holy One.
    How grand their faith as they proclaimed
The future glory of the Church, o'er which the Father
  • and the Son
Were watching with such lofty purpose, that man,
Unless his eyes were touched by power divine

Could scarce conceive.
Still other centuries were born and died,
And God still lived;
The sun and moon obeyed his high behest,
And then the sweet old chapters tell,
How one, who heard the morning stars
When first they sang,
Who since had dwelt in heavenly clime,
Came freely down to earth, dwelling in low estate,
And humble way, and mingled with his fellow-men,
And healed their sick, and gave them bread,
Gave vision to the blind, and brought to life the dead;
And at the last by yielding life itself,
Made plain the way, by which all men
Might find eternal life.
And how our hearts exult as other pages tell,
How he, the Son of God,
Conquered the grave and death,
Passing as we must pass through gates of flesh,
Received as we may be through privilege he bought
To life eternal unalloyed by sin.
And so each leaf of the old book is dear,
From the first page yellow with time,

On which is traced a name
Long since exchanged for grander title,
    Such as angels use,
Until we reach the closing chapter,
    Telling of the "city," of whose glory
Heart can not conceive, a home prepared
    And made at fearful cost;
A heritage for those who come with robes made white,
And hearts made pure, through the shed blood of
    Christ,
To claim the royal gifts, home, life eternal, rest, and
    peace.

Here and There.

WE are drifting toward the Eden,
    Over on the other shore.
    Clouds and darkness are about us;
    There, no clouds for evermore.

Here, we're tossed upon life's billows;
    There, we'll rest without a fear.

Here, we sorrow for lost treasures;
    There, each treasure will be near.

Now we mourn for joys departed,
    In our blindness and our pain,
Hardly thinking that the Savior
    Can restore them all again.

In that home beyond the river,
    Where the good and pure have flown,
We shall have such glad reunions,
    Close beside the Father's throne.

Then our "light afflictions" ended,
    Nothing more to dread or fear,
Loving eyes, and loving hand-clasps,
    The dear Savior ever near.

Rest, my soul, in patience waiting,
    The glad hour is just at hand,
When the welcome, "Come up higher,"
    Bids us to the "promised land."

An Old-Time Memory.

A Memory of the Olden Time.

N a hill-top, in the east land,
  Spreading west, and south, and northward,
    Spreading wide its lovely pastures,
And its meadows green and fragrant,
Far from distant town or city,
Lay a homestead clothed in beauty;
With its orchards fair to look at,
And its ripe fruits sweet to taste of,
Apples, pears, and golden peaches,
Rich and spicy, as the nectar
Quaffed by gods in the days olden.
All the hedges draped and vine-clad,
Home of bird and haunt of squirrel;
And the graceful elms and maples,
With their wealth of leaves and branches,
Sheltered many a feathered songster,
Who poured forth such perfect music
That the ear was charmed to listen,
And the heart was lifted higher,

8

By the blending of their voices.
Here and there the cattle rested
'Neath the overhanging branches,
Or, along the murmuring streamlet,
Nipped the blossoms of the clover;
While the lambs, with nimble footsteps,
Skipped, and ran, and played together.
Clothed they were in soft, white raiment,
Pure and white as driven snow-flakes,
Emblem of the Lamb once offered
For the sins of all the nations.

Nestled down in this Arcadia
Was a plain and homely cottage,
Built of logs, and chinked with plaster;
And, about the eaves and corners,
Climbed the hop-vine and the creeper;
And the pretty morning-glory
Wound its tendrils o'er the windows,
Creeping on around the door-case,
Smiling in its wealth of beauty,
At the dawning of the morning,
Nodding, as the breezes passed it,
Laden with the early bird-song,

Or the hum of bee or insect.
Grouped upon the mossy carpet
Of the smooth and ample door-yard
Were the roses, red and royal;
Damask roses, bright and royal,
As when sunlight, toward the evening,
Decks the west in colors gorgeous.

The old well, with oaken bucket,
With its mossy curb and well-sweep,
With its pure and cooling waters,
Sweet and pure refreshing waters,
Stood within an easy distance
From the little homely cottage.
In and out, within the doorway,
To the well, and to the garden—
Where the green corn shook its tassels,
Where the peas and young potatoes,
Where the camomile and sage-bed,
And the rue and bitter wormwood,
Side by side grew close together,
Went the mistress of the cottage,
Smiling at the gorgeous flowers,
Brilliant poppies and nasturtions,

Marigolds and flaming sunflowers—
Gathering now and then sweet clover,
A few rosebuds and some violets;
And she tied them up with grasses,
As she hastened to the corner
Where were tangled berry bushes.
Soon her little basket filling
With black-caps and scarlet berries,
Back she went along the border,
Past the plum-trees richly laden
With their fruit, both brown and golden—
Fruit from trees she brought from Jersey,
In the years when loving husband
Walked beside her, bearing burdens,
Ere the sod grew green above him.

As she pauses at the door-stone,
Where the latch-string hangs inviting,
We accept her kindly greeting,
Pass with her into the door-way,
At her bidding take the large chair—
Brought from England in the old-time—
With its high back brightly polished,
Smooth and glossy like a mirror,

Heir-loom in that cottage humble.
Then Katrina, the home-mother,
Placed the berries on the dresser—
On the quaint and shining dresser—
By the row of pewter platters,
Bright as moonbeams on the waters,
Or the silver spoons beside them,
Were the platters of the housewife.
Then she took the bunch of flowers
Tied with grasses from the basket,
Placed them in a vase of china
Brought by grandsire o'er the waters ;
Put the vase upon the bureau,
By the candlesticks so curious,
Made of fine brass, tall and stately.
Then, with deft and nimble fingers,
She was busy for a season,
Busy with her household duties.
Back and forth to cleanly milk-room,
With its rich and creamy flavor,
Where were rolls of golden butter,
And the odor of the pastures
From the clean white wooden buckets,

And the milk-jars ranged about her.
    While she worked and sang together
Glanced my eyes about the cottage,
Saw the beds piled high like snow-drifts;
Saw the curtains hung about them,
Made of chintz, with bird and flower
Scattered o'er them, a rare pattern—
Blue the birds, and blue the flowers,
Laid upon a pure, white background.
And the cottage walls were whitewashed,
And the tiny windows curtained
With a little snowy curtain,
Large enough to make an apron
For a dainty little maiden.
And, across the room, a carpet,
Warp of yarn, and rags for filling,
Striped with red, and green, and yellow,
Fresh and cheerful, bright to look at.
Strewn with sand, in dainty patterns,
Was the white floor just beyond it,
Sand brought from the great white sand-stone,
That lay broken in the pasture.
Then, like work in art mosaic,

Lay the broad and friendly hearth-stone;
And the fire-place, wide and roomy,
With its cheerful fire just kindled,
Large enough to boil the kettle
Which sang out its homely welcome.
And the firelight laughed and shimmered,
Climbed the chimney to the old crane ;
Threw its bright light o'er the andirons,
With their queer and grotesque moldings ;
Laughed and chattered as the smoke-cloud,
Wreathed in masses, climbed the chimney,
Seeking home with air and sunlight.
     Then Katrina sat beside me,
Smoothed her brow and coiled her dark hair,
Fastened it with stately shell-comb ;
Smoothed her dress of home-spun linen,
Placed o'er all a snowy apron
Made of flax of her own spinning ;
Round her neck a dainty kerchief,
Gift of loved and absent brother.
Then she told me of her home life ;
Of the dear one long since buried ;
Of her sons so good and tender ;

Of her daughters, one a widow ;
And her dear old gray-haired mother,
Whose years numbered many a decade.
Then, with reverence, she mentioned
The dear friend, the Elder Brother,
Who had always stood beside her ;
Who had always smoothed her pathway ;
Who had kept her feet from falling,
And upheld her heart from fainting.
And she told me of her purpose,
If her years were few or many,
To rely upon his goodness,
Trust his promises forever,
Though her days be few or many.
      And I loved the good Katrina ;
And bethought me of the priestess,
And the oracles of old days,
To whom messengers from all lands,
Came to get inspired answers.
And I knew this loving daughter,
Faithful wife, and tender mother,
Was a priestess, was inspired ;
Did her life-work well and nobly,

Would be crowned and would be honored—
Here on earth by those who love her,
And in heaven a crown more precious
Than the diadem of priestess
Would bedeck her brow immortal.

<hr />

A Sermon on Canvas.

THE afternoon was warm, hardly a breath of air was stirring; the room where I was writing seemed close, although the windows were open and the door stood ajar.

I began to feel conscious of weariness ; my brain did not respond to the promptings of my will, and my hands moved unwillingly over the paper. I looked out through the open windows, hoping to get inspiration from the lovely view that opened out before me—of woods, and lake, harvest fields, and orchards, with their wealth of fruitage ; but they all looked sleepy and warm and dusty.

Even the busy bees seemed less busy than usual,

and the flies were droning lazily about. All nature seemed in sympathy, and I could not resist the influence; and, leaning back in my easy-chair, yielded to the spirit of the hour. Glancing up after a few moments, my eyes rested upon a beautiful picture, a gift from a dear friend. It was a quiet landscape, done in oil and tastefully framed.

I had always admired it, and at times had felt its soothing influence, but to-day it had a new strange power over me.

In the foreground was a moss-grown log ; it was such a log as I had used for a seat many a time when, as a child, I explored the forest depths. Close beside it was a grassy mound that sloped away to a border of little trees and shrubs, and I knew the busy water laved their roots, although it was hidden from my sight by the dense foliage.

And so I followed along the pretty stream, a child again, sailing my little boats, or wading out into the cool waters to pick up the white pebbles, watching the little minnows as they darted about, glad and happy.

By and by the stream broadened, and at length gave itself, with song and laughter, into the bosom of a little lake, whose waters, smooth and clear, mirrored surrounding objects.

It was a lovely view, the crystal lake framed in by trees, and rocks, dells, and waterfalls, and towering mountains, whose tops were flooded with golden sunlight, while here and there the drifting rays glorified branch, or tree, or flower. And so I wandered on, climbing mossy banks, or resting in shaded nooks ; drinking from gurgling fountains, half hidden by ferns and wildwood grasses, or refreshing myself with the juicy berries ; and I said truly, ''Books in the running brooks, sermons in stones, and good in every thing.''

But the mountains in the background had for me the greater charm, as they lifted themselves above and beyond, each higher than the last, growing more attractive as the distance seemed greater, until at last I thought they might really be the '' Delectable Mountains,'' and that the ''city whose builder and maker is God'' was just beyond. And so the warm afternoon slipped away, and I found myself rested and refreshed by this '' Sermon on Canvas,'' for which an appropriate text might have been, ''The works of the Lord are great.''

A Christmas Poem.

IN thought we wander back through eighteen cen-
    turies,
        And find ourselves on Ephrath's height,
O'erlooking the Judean hills and vales.
The city, now called the house of bread,
Builded by Israel's sweet singer,
        Is placed upon its brow;
While all about are olive groves and vineyards rare,
        And just beyond are fruitful vales,
        And grassy slopes,
Where flocks and herds of the Judean shepherds
        Find green pastures.

        Through these same valleys,
And along the base of loftier hills,
A little farther on, the youthful David
Kept his sheep in years long past.
And here the wondrous prayers
And psalms of praise were written,
While he walked and talked with God;
        But in this crowning year,

The Annunciation of the Angel.

When God's great plan to save the world
    Should be complete,
Not one, but many shepherds lead their flocks
Beside cool springs, or to the shaded dells,
    For food and rest.

They love their work, for even the air
    Is filled with notes of joy,
And blade of grass, and rock, and rill,
Find each a voice, by which to utter thanks.
The shepherds often speak of Christ,
    The promised one,
And wonder if the prophet's words will soon come true;
When he, the child of hope,
The wonderful, the mighty God, the Prince of peace,
    Would come to reign.
And so abounding is their faith,
That from each heart the cry is echoed back,
    "The Lord doth reign! Let earth rejoice!"

Night spreads its mantle o'er the land.
The flocks, obedient to their leaders' call,
    Are safe within the fold.
Each shepherd seeks his favorite resting place,

Where he may watch and wait for break of day,
Communing much with God,
Or speaking of the ways by which he led
His chosen ones in other years.
Suddenly from out the darkness
Comes an angel of the Lord,
And all about the angel is the glory
Like that which rested on the mount,
When God was there to speak to Israel's host.

So bright the heavenly vision,
That the shepherds feared and trembled,
Until the angel speaks.
"Fear not," he said,
"I bring you tidings of great joy,
For unto you is born, this day, in David's town,
A Savior, which is Christ the Lord!"
And then a host from out the courts of heaven,
With one voice, sang the chorus,
Which every nation, tongue, and tribe shall oft repeat,
Until from pole to pole, and shore to shore,
The glad harmonious echo shall resound,
"Glory to God on high! Peace be on earth!
Good will to man!"

The Hour of Prayer.

WRITTEN AT THE HOUR SET APART FOR PRAYER FOR THE CONVERSION OF
HEATHEN WOMEN.

IT is the hour of prayer, and many an earnest Chris-
        tian
    Now hastens to the quiet place where God is found,
To ask that he would save and bless the multitude
        Who know him not—
A wondrous throng of zealous workers,
Who have sought and found the way of life;
And, knowing that it is a path of peace,
        They can not rest
    Until the dark-skinned wives and mothers,
    Dwelling in lands beyond the sea,
Shall also find the Savior, who for them
        Gave up his precious life.

How each heart throbs with thankfulness
    For Bibles, and for Christian homes,
For faithful teachers, and for all the helps
    Which we, a favored nation, have
    To aid us in the heavenward way.

And while we tell the Savior all our wants
　　The memory of many a prayer,
Offered perhaps with trembling lips and flowing tears,
　　Yet mixed with faith,
　　Has brought to us such peace and comfort
　　As only Christ can give.

　　And so we come in confidence,
Knowing that if but two or three shall ask aright,
　　The promise is to them,
　　And when a chorus of *many* voices
　　Join in this most sacred hour
To ask the precious boon, that all for whom Christ died
　　Might hear his voice and seek his face,
　　We dare not doubt but God will hear;
　　And so we come and ask,
That Thine inheritance may spread,
Until the heathen tribes are gathered
　　To the knowledge of the truth.

May thy possessions reach to distant fields,
And may all forms of idol worship be destroyed,
　　And, in its place, a knowledge
　　Of thy law, thy love, and the great truths

That are the outgrowth of thine own shed blood,
> Shall form a center,
> Round which the nations who have dwelt
> In darkness and in shadow
> Shall rally to the light and glory
Which the Sun of righteousness, alone, imparts.

> And may we further ask,
> That the dear sisters scattered far and near,
> O'er this great mission field,
As they come up, a mighty host,
May so besiege a throne of grace,
With faith persistent and united,
> That thou wilt hear?
And, as when Daniel plead with thee at evening's hour,
> An angel came to him and said,
"Thy supplication has been heard, and the command-
> ment has gone forth,
> For thou art well beloved,"
So may this praying band be strengthened by thy words,
> And made more steadfast in the truth
> That all the world shall be subdued to thee.

9

The Lord Pitieth them that Fear Him.

THE marvelous care of the Father,
    To those who abide in his love,
The pity he cheerfully giveth,
    Had its birth in the kingdom above.

If sickness falls on such as fear him,
    How gladly he comforteth them,
If one he has chosen has fallen,
    He raiseth him up again.

And if one offend in his weakness,
    And sorrow for what he has done,
If he comes to the Lord in submission,
    He'll receive the penitent one.

And should one be wronged by another,
    The promise is certainly made,
That the unlawful bonds shall be broken,
    If he come to the Lord for aid.

And 'tis thus with every trial,
    That's permitted on us to fall,
For he pitieth them that fear him,
    His protection is over all.

The Mother of Abraham Lincoln.

REMOVAL FROM THE OLD HOME, DEATH, BURIAL, AND LATER FUNERAL SERVICES.

 HOUSEHOLD group had left their early home;
O'er hill and dale, through forest shade they roamed,
And found themselves among strange scenes alone.

They built a cottage on the prairie wide,
And planted vines its loneliness to hide,
Trying to feel they would be satisfied.

Neighbors were few, and lived so far away
That, in their loneliness, they oft did say
" We have not seen a human face to-day."

Two years had passed away, and, in that time,
A few had sought and found the favored clime,
And pitched their tents where woodland flowers twine.

Disease had followed in their train;
The mother lay prostrate on couch of pain,
'T was feared she ne'er would rise again.

Her heart more tender grew each day,
She felt how brief her earthly stay,
And spoke quite often of the holier way.

The son beloved, her special care,
Who largely in her thoughts did share,
Oft listened to her evening prayer

That in his youth he might begin
To shun the paths of guilt and sin
And strive eternal life to win.

The grateful son read words of life,
Of freedom from the toil and strife,—
And then she died, the cherished wife.

A few friends came; her grave was made
'Neath forest trees, under whose shade
Sweet flowers bloomed, soft breezes played.

The little home was left forlorn,
The hands that once its walls adorned
Were folded close that Summer morn.

But, when the evening shadows fell,
The sorrowing ones used oft to tell
Of virtues they remembered well.

' They mourned above her tomb unblessed
By Gospel sermon, song of rest,
And wondered if the one loved best

Would come and speak above her grave
Of final rest, God's power to save,
Of Christ, the precious gift the Father gave.

Time sped away; the son had penned
A letter, which he planned to send
To Pastor Elken, the mother's friend.

For many a day the sun had come and gone,
And anxious thoughts came to the loving son—
The way was long, the pastor might not come.

But, at the twilight hour, one sought
A shelter in their humble cot,
And wondered that they knew him not.

And as his hand they kindly pressed,
He spoke of her, the truly blessed,
And of the approaching day of rest

When he would meet in forest shade
The friends she loved, from hill and glade,
Who would gather where her grave was made.

From near and far they hastened there,
The sorrows of these friends to share,
And listen to the good man's prayer.

He spoke of her young life so pure,
Of precious truths to her made sure,
And of God's Word that would endure.

And many a mourner bowed the head
Above her green and narrow bed,
And bitter were the tears they shed.

At length, the solemn service done,
Last words spoken o'er the buried one,
All had gone, except the son,

Who, while the tears bedewed his face,
Asked, at the last, to have a place
Near her he loved through power of grace.

He vowed his mother's God's to serve,
And ne'er from duty's call would swerve
If kingly power his arm would nerve.

And truthfully he kept his word,
No sinful thought his bosom stirred,
Nor evil act of his was heard.

And when at last the nation chose
That he should stand against her foes
And tide of evil should oppose,

He faltered not, but, in that hour,
With shield of faith, God's help his tower,
Went forth, in majesty of power,

To break the chains from the oppressed,
To help earth's lowly ones to rest:
His home to find among the blest.

An Afternoon at the Ferry.

ONE pleasant September day, while traveling with a
dear friend by private conveyance, it was our pleasure to cross, by "ferry," one of the lovely lakes
for which central New York is justly noted, and, in the
early afternoon, we found ourselves at the "landing"—
a picturesque spot, with its few homes dropped about
at the foot of high hills, which served as background
to the pretty scene.

Giant trees added to the beauty and gave needful
shade.   Our eyes followed the long stretch of water in
its graceful undulation, with its sparkle and shimmer, as
the sun rays touched it here and there, until in the distance it was framed in wooded banks or fruitful harvest
fields.

The boat was far down on the other shore, and was
signaled to return.   In the mean time a basket of
grapes, "ripe and royal," was found, and we feasted in
the fullest sense, for eye and heart were fed by the
beauty about us.   In a little time a carriage approached
the landing, a roomy, hospitable carriage, and it was
"full to the brim."

It seemed to be a family party—consisting of father,
mother, a maiden sister of the wife, one would think
from the likeness, and a group of round-faced, happy
children.   The plainness of their attire revealed their
faith, for the ladies wore the quaint Quaker bonnets,
and plain rich dresses in modest colors.   Their faces
were quiet, restful faces.   Smooth and fresh, one could
not trace the lines of care, and their rich glossy hair did
not even hint at the approach of age.   The husband and
father was evidently "a good man and true."   For his

broad hat covered a kindly face, and his straight coat was not a prophecy of narrow sympathies, as his abundant care of his household testified.

We were much interested, especially in the children, demure little maidens they were, with not a "kink or curl," their rosy faces shaded by close bonnets, their childish forms arrayed in plain fitting waists and gathered skirts, guiltless of gore, tuck, or ruffle. They looked glad and happy, and "thee" and "thou" fell from their lips as naturally as if they had used the musical pronouns for many years. Soon another carriage came, and still others, laden with members of the same "household of faith," until it seemed if others should come, a new element (close communion) might be mingled with their lives, if not with their faith.

They were a companionable people, and explained to us that they were returning from a "quarterly meeting," held on the opposite side of the lake from their settlement. They told us of their thrifty homes, of the prosperous school they supported, of their industry and almost uniform health, of the success which had crowned their efforts as a community, until it almost seemed as if the dream of an "Arcadia" had been realized.

The last carriage had reached the "point" just as
the boat touched the landing, and there was hurry and
bustle until horses and carriages were safely stowed,
and the people gathered in congenial groups, and the
boat was again under motion, ·headed for the other
shore.

Separated a little from the rest were the young people, and among them a few "boys" from the "out-
side," who, we were told, were members of their
school, had come to study the languages under their
capable teacher; but as we noticed their interest in the
fair girls, and saw their drifting color at the delicate at-
tentions paid them by the boys, we fancied they were
all learning a language sweeter far than Greek or Latin,
a living language; spoken, not by tongue alone, but
glance and touch are its interpreters.

Among the pleasant things that were drifting to me
through all that pleasant day, I was conscious at last
of another element, a little feeling of discomfort, for,
although not given to "frizzes or flounces," yet my
traveling dress, so tasteful in the morning. began to
seem elaborate in contrast with the stately plainness of
my fellow-travelers, and the simple flower on my hat

took on large proportions. The words I had often read, about the " ornament of a meek and quiet spirit," came knocking at the door of memory, and, as an aid in dismissing the thought, I addressed myself to a comely woman, referring to her children and the varied duties of life, speaking at last of her apparent health and freshness, to which she replied it was owing largely to her freedom from the thralldom of fashion in dress, and quite unconsciously gave me a little sermon on the subject of which I had been thinking. Our trip was nearly ended and my convictions were stifled for the time.

As the shadows lengthened we reached the harbor, and, hastening arrangements, were soon seated in the carriage, listening to the kind farewells of our Quaker friends, whose homes were in another direction from our own destination. Among the September days we have placed this pleasant memory of the afternoon at the ferry.

The Early Called.

FOR two short years
Our hearts were gladdened
By the presence of our little son.
In memory he lingers with us still.
The glow of health is on his cheek,
His eyes are brilliant with the light of happy childhood,
While his busy little feet
Go with me in my daily rounds;
His voice, so full of music, lingers in my ear,
And fills me with a sort of quiet joy
As I remember
All his childish thoughts,
And wants so sweetly told.
Again, I see him wrestling with disease.
His fevered cheek and labored breath
Betoken intense pain.
Dear friends come to his side with outstretched hands
And ready sympathy—
Parents so love their only son,
That they would barter years of life

To bring him rest again.
An only sister, who has cared for him
　　Through all his tender years,
　　　　Weeps such agonizing tears
As might almost recall the dead to life.
But all in vain.　The Father claims his own,
　　　　And we must yield him up.

　　　.　　.　　.　　.　　.　　.　　.

　　　Morn dawns, but brings no ray of hope ;
The little feet are swiftly speeding
　　　　Toward death's river,
　　　And soon we stand with him upon its banks
And look across.　We see the shore all verdure lined,
　　　　And dotted here and there
　　　With ever blooming flowers.
　　　　We see the waters—
Not dark and turbid, as we feared,
　　　　But clear and limpid—
Rippling over pearls and precious stones,
And radiant with the light reflected from the Temple
　　of our God.
　　　We may not go with him as we had hopes,
　　　But linger, watching the little bark,

Until we see it moored close by the port of heaven.
    Familiar faces hover near,
   Ready to take, with reverent touch,
The new-born angel to the Savior's breast,
The while they chant, "Saved from the power of sin,
    Redeemed through love divine."
We watch them through the blinding tears,
    Until the golden gates are reached;
      And as they pass from sight
We catch such glimpses of the better land,
That we, too, wish we might be clothed in white,
    "And be accounted worthy."
   Not yet we hear the summons,
    So we place our hands
Over our aching hearts and whisper,
    "He may not come to us,
   But we, through power of grace,
    Will go to him."

A Cherry-tree in Bloom.

THIS lovely May day, as the breezes play,
    Through the broad, low, cherry-tree,
  With its brow alight, with the drifting white—
    Can it be that it blooms for me?

Does it mean to bless with its offering pure,
    Like a poem or song unsung?
And what is the story 'twould breathe in my ear,
    If it had a voice and a tongue?

Would it speak of the force, the air and light,
    That feed and nourish its frame,
The old brown earth, its power and might,
    And the dew, and the soft falling rain?

Would it tell of the hand that crowned it with flowers,
    And filled them with fragrance rare?
If any were like them in Eden's bowers,
    They seem so perfect and fair.

The little bees hum, as like fairies they flit
    Through the clusters so green and white,

And honey from one and another they sip,
　　Their little lives full of delight.

The birds come and go in a joyous way,
　　As they build up their little nest,
In the depth of bloom where the shadows play,
　　Where the dear little birdlings will rest.

Is the "tree of life" on the other shore,
　　In beauty more perfect or pure?
We only know this is drifting away,
　　While that will forever endure.

Earth's Music.

G O with me to the dark old woods,
　　And sit you down beneath that leafy arch,
　　Upon the moss-grown log, and listen.
Ah! here comes the low-toned zephyr,
Gently murmuring in your ear,
And finds an answering echo in your heart,
As in varied notes it breathes of that great power

Earth's Music.

Which gave it birth.   The infinite choir
Of little songsters tune their sweetest notes,
All joining in a song of praise, so full of melody,
So varied, yet so rich and perfect as a whole,
That if we close our eyes it makes us dream of heaven.
Each chorus and duet is full of harmony,
While waving tree-top, and timid flower,
And grassy spire, keep time to nature's music.
                    The murmuring rill
Gently warbles its soft evening song,
As musically it ripples by, and then perchance
The notes are varied, as with swifter motion
It onward speeds to join the world of waters.
There's music's richest strain in ocean's roar,
And in the wildest howlings of the wind,
And the trumpet tongues of towering mountains,
For God is speaking through them in his matchless power.
The voice of God is concentrated power of song,
And as it rests upon the ear it fills the heart
With joyous images; then is the time
To lift our thoughts above in grateful prayer,
Which will be caught by listening angels,
And again re-echoed through the arch of heaven.

The voice of prayer is music that vibrates
From heart to heart, and even Deity is pleased,
And graciously accepts the incense of the soul.

Through Watkins Glen.

WE tarry for a while
     Within this vestibule of mysteries,
     While o'er our hearts steal premonitions
     Of grandeur unrevealed,
Which but for handiwork of man
Would still be shut away from mortal eye.
     Above, around, in half circumference,
     Are towering walls, which almost meet,
     Save for a narrow rift,
As if some mighty power had rent the rocks
     From out an angle.
     More than threescore feet above,
A thread of water dashes downward
     To a pool of unknown depth,
Where finny tribes disport themselves in glee;

Here nature with daintiest device
Has frescoed the gray walls
With ferns and ivy vines and wildwood flowers,
And wealth of shade, in tree and shrub,
So varied, yet so perfect,
That we scarce can leave the restful picture,
But would gladly take it with us
Through our lives.
We tear ourselves away at last,
Passing in "Glen Alpha's" open door,
And climb to heights above,
Resting awhile upon a little bridge
That spans the chasm.
Looking back through jagged rocks,
To deep blue waters, broken into circles
By the falling column in its quick descent,
An upward glance
Reveals a wondrous sight.
Towering cliffs of dark old rocks,
Sullen and angular, rise far above each other,
Till they appear to meet the clouds.
Just beyond the way seems hedged
By stony battlements,

But glancing round an abrupt turn,
We find where steps are cut in stone,
　　Leading 'neath overhanging cliff,
Along a narrow gorge, by quiet water-flow.
　　Around and overhead are rocks,
　　With varied hues and tints,
With abrupt angles, and eccentric curves,
As if dame Nature here had robed herself
　　In most grotesque array.
　　A little farther on a beautiful cascade,
　　　　Irregular, yet full of grace,
Its waters broken in their fall,
　　　　Dashes along,
　　Throwing its foam and spray,
And still goes laughing on its joyous way.
Another "fairy cascade" with bound and leap
Casts itself in trusting way in "Neptune's pool."
Onward we see the grandeur unsurpassed,
　　　　Of "cavern gorge,"
　　As through the labyrinth,
　　Still under shelving cliffs,
　　We pass into a "grotto," damp and dark,
　　　Shut in behind a watery veil,

The roar of which is echoed by the rocky walls,
    While outer lights
    Touch the transparent stream
With flecks like molten silver.
Backward, a little way, and then
We climb and rest, and climb again,
Not daring to look down, until
    The dizzy height is reached.
From this, our lofty perch, we look
Through "vista" of quiet pools, and silvery cascades,
At stately walls, with garnishing of moss,
Flooded with light from cloudless skies.
    Still above are stately trees,
    Clothed in their varied shades,
From palest tint, to darkest evergreen,
    Amid whose shimmering leaves
    The sun rays dart and gleam
    In fashion all their own.
Rested, we climb again, reaching a point
Where, hid among the nooks and corners,
We see a vegetation which the tropics claim;
Or just across, where keen north winds
    Find southern cliffs.

Are lichens, from the northern zones.
A little higher still, we see
A dainty cottage, perched upon a natural shelf.
The view is unsurpassed, "the half can not be told,"
Yet one might find enough of beauty here
To sweeten half a life.
We tarry for a while, for man with thought ingenious,
Has fashioned homes on liberal plan,
And spread them out on breezy hill-side,
Or built them high
Above unmeasured depths,
Where all the wants of life are met in hospitable way.
The North and South, the East and West,
The islands of the sea, contribute
Of their choice and pleasant things
To minister to earthly wants,
Or satisfy the broader need of mind or heart.
Here, too, we find a strong,
Yet dainty network o'er the chasm,
Founded on ledge of rock, so deep
That thought can hardly reach the place,
Or touch the time
Away among the centuries,

When its foundation stones were laid.
    So harmonius the accord
        Of art and nature,
It almost seems as if the two had met
    In long communion, to devise,
And carry out, in loving emulation,
Plans by which each might reveal
        The other's charm.
    But other beauties beckon,
And we hasten on, through "Sylvan gorge,"
    'Neath arches made of forest trees,
    With vine-clad cliffs on either hand.
A hundred feet above, on jutting crag,
A rustic arbor stands, close by a gallery of art,
    Where many a treasured gem is hidden,
Copied by skillful hands from lands remote, or near,
    Fair landscapes painted under eastern skies,
Or lordly mountain view from western slope,
        So true to nature
    That they seem an echo of her voice.
Still downward over mossy slopes
        That crown the chasm,
Feasting our eyes on "Diamond Fall,"

A lovely picture,
Framed in forest, rock, and stream,
        We pause beside a group
    Of tiny rapids and cascades,
That dance, and leap, and frolic,
Like happy children in their merry moods.

Just here the great "cathedral" stands,
The lofty temple wrought in silence most profound,
Where thousands yearly come on willing pilgrimage.
Its walls five hundred span in height,
        Its roof the archivault of heaven,
            Reflected in the crystal pools
            That sprinkle its vast floor,
            As if huge pearls were dropped
            Between the great gray stones,
To catch and multiply the golden sunbeams,
Or the quiet rays the pale moon gives,
Or dainty jets from countless hosts of stars,
That march in stately way across the sky.
            Here, too, is the "baptismal font,"
            Whose radiant waters, clear and pure,
                Reveal the smallest object
                Resting in their depths.

And here is music from waterfalls that never tire,
But with their solemn chant,
Varied by lighter song,
Continue through the years their notes of praise.
We bow our heads,
Our hearts are filled with awe,
And it seems fitting we should offer sacrifice;
And as we stand within this temple,
Builded, perchance, when time was young,
And try to comprehend the thought
That fashioned it,
Our poor humanity in contrast seems
Like grain of sand, or water drop from ocean's depths.

We leave unwillingly, but find a charm
In watching foaming waters
Find their way adown a path of sixty feet.
The "matchless scene" next meets our eye,
Where beauties manifold combine.
Here rock and rill
Shake hands with pools and seething rapids,
While winding channels and cascades,
Attune their voices to united harmony,
And sky and foliage smile down upon

The friendly group;
The "triple cascades," lovely in union,
Yet unlike, possess a nameless charm.
    We pass behind the "Rainbow Falls,"
    Where myriad drops, and tiny threads
Of water, falling from shelving rocks above,
    Break into mist and form a veil,
Through which the sun reveals a rainbow,
    With her paler sister by her side,
A prophecy of God's unchanging Word.
        We pass through "Shadow Gorge,"
        And by the "Emerald Pool,"
        Around the "Frowning Cliff,"
        And hasten to do homage at the "Pillar,"
        Crowned with beauty.
    So charming is this place
It seems as if some tasteful hand
    Had gathered treasures choice,
And brought them to inweave in crevice,
And o'er columns of solid masonry.
        Our eyes feast next
Upon the "Artist's Dream," "Arcadia of the Glens,"
Where pools, and angles, light and shade,

And dainty curves, and silver sheen commingle,
As if choice samples from the other glens
    Were gathered in,
  To decorate this lovely spot.
We pass the "Pool of Nymphs," where water sprites
Hold levees in the sunny afternoons;
And on with ease to "Glen Facility,"
Whose walls are held in place
By a great iron bridge, a wondrous work,
    Impressing us with power of mind,
    That bends the hills and lifts the valleys up
      To meet man's will.
Beyond the bridge, "Glen Horicon,"
With ampitheater, and wooded banks,
    And broken points of land,
    Ending in "Glen Elysium,"
    With water, lawn, and grove,
With cosy nooks, and carpetings of moss,
    And giant trees o'er all.
Next "Glen Omega," last of all, reveals its charms,
Three miles away from Alpha's open door,
Six hundred feet above the entrance way.
    And as we wait and strive

In little knowledge, or by power of thought,
To solve the mystery of the birth and later life
Of this great marvel of creative power,
We lose ourselves, and only by flight of fancy
    Can look back through space of time,
When earth was new, and called complete,
    And think within this secret place
Might have been left the unused rock and stone—
Not as a blight on the fair earth—
    For all God's works were good.
Later, when nature, handmaid of the architect
    That framed the world,
Had draped the mountains, planted forests wide,
    Sown varied wealth
    O'er the vast plains of earth,
Dropped ferns and mosses in her vales,
    And by the river's brink—
For large provision had been made—
She, too, had overplus of wealth,
And poured into these nooks and corners
    The unused seeds and shrubs,
        And little roots,
With thought prophetic of their future life.

The little birds
Told all the tale to other birds,
And so from distant points
They now and then would bring a tiny seed,
To drop within its depths.
And as the breezes roamed abroad
They breathed the secret,
And the feathery seeds came on their wings,
And fell on mossy bed, or lodged in rift of rock,
And grew, and waved in triumph
At their own success.
Melted snows, and mountain streams,
And rills, and drops of dew,
Listened with curious ear,
And came at last to see,
Bringing their pretty offerings.
On tallest cliffs, the eagles perched,
To watch the changes wrought from year to year,
Until at last
Man dared to scale the dizzy height,
And seek the lower depths,
Explore the darkest nooks,
And bring its hidden beauties forth,

Its old-time majesty, perhaps unchanged,
Yet clothed upon with fresher charm,
    As if the resurrection power
    Had touched and purified.
And so to-day the tongue of man, and nature's voice,
    Accord with voice of God,
    Who in creation's morn
    Pronounced it "very good."

The Voice of many Waters.

WE have heard the voice, the still small voice,
    Of the gentle Summer rain,
  As it watered the earth with refreshing showers,
    Reviving all nature again.

We have heard the rills, as they wind along
    Through vale, and meadow, and grove,
And they sparkle and laugh as they sing their **song,**
    Their beautiful song of love.

We have heard the voice of the waterfall,
    As it dashes adown the hill,

And it almost seemed it might have said,
    I will hasten to do thy will.

We have seen the river as it walks in pride
    On its way toward the ocean broad;
With its voice it praises the hand that guides,
    'T is the wonderful hand of God.

And the beautiful lake, with its border of green,
    With a cloudless sky o'erhead,
Reflected in waves of silvery sheen,
    In the depths of its crystal bed,

Seem to speak of the river of life above,
    Making glad the home of the pure,
Where provision is made for one and for all
    Who in patience and faith shall endure.

We have heard the roar of the ocean grand,
    Like the voice from Sinai's height,
And it tells of One holding the waves in his hands,
    Who dwelleth forever in light.

Wayside Flowers.

WE love the way-side flowers,
For they are free to all ;
The simple daisies, with their yellow hearts and
pearly fringe,
Were made by the same hand that fashioned rare
exotics,
And lift themselves as gracefully
To greet the passer-by, as do their prouder sisters.
And one might almost think the buttercups, so glossy
and so golden,
Were fed and nourished at the springs
That send the sunshine forth.
The clover, red and white, is strewn about,
Holding its hidden sweets on hospitable thought intent,
For busy bees unchided come and go,
Carrying their store of Winter food.
Along the bank the creeping blackberry
Winds among the grass,
Looking as if its star-shaped blooms
Had been in careless fashion dropped.

While they cling close to earth, as bashful children
   That hold fast the mother's hand.
      Gay dandelions
Gather in groups to greet the passer-by with their
   coquettish smile,
   And still seem happy, as their early beauty fades,
   To wear their silver locks, a type of riper age.
The rare sweet-brier, hiding among the nooks and
   corners,
     Has its word of love and sympathy,
For, as we look upon its modest face,
   And breathe the grateful incense,
It seems like tender touch of old-time friend,
Bringing sweet memories of childhood days.
    And so we love the wayside flowers,
    Which, like the air we breathe,
Or the pure waters from the mountain-stream,
    Bless rich and poor alike.

11

The Mighty Word.

"So mightily grew the Word of God and prevailed."—
Acts xix, 20.

THE mighty Word,
 Expressive of the thoughts more mighty
  Than the words convey to human ear,—
   For written words are tame
Beside the thoughts of God toward all his creatures,
  Thoughts which had their birth
   In the great heart of Him
  Who was, and is, and shall forever be;
  Thoughts of the gift of life eternal
   To his chosen ones,
Who are thus made to share his immortality,—
And so his Word, with mercy and with justice fraught,
  Grew and prevailed.
As tiny oak, by innate strength, turns obstacles aside,
  Pressing its way through the moist earth,
  Until it revels in the sunshine and the air,
   Still stretching out its arms,
   Gathering fresh power each day,

Until it towers above its fellows,
Defying storm and tempest,
So the Word, rooted and grounded, did prevail.

The combined forces of the heathen world
That numbered in its countless hosts
Emperors, and kings, and hordes of willing devotees,
With varied forms of idol worship,
Worship of wood, or stone, beast, bird, or fowl,
Or sacred waters, could not prevail against the Word
of God.
Even those who bowed in adoration to the sun,
That marvel of creative power,
Must yield their final homage
To the Hand that hung it in the heavens.
And as time passed.
And the great powers of earth in solemn conclave met,
And asked the mighty question, "Shall the Word of
God prevail?
His name be honored, and his cross revered?"
The glad triumphant answer,
"He the God of nations is,"
Made all his foes to quake and flee away
To hide themselves; and so the Word prevailed.

Judaism, which for centuries had grown,
Sustained and strengthened by its old-time rites,
    On whose red altars blood of beasts
    Was freely shed, to atone for sin,
Arrayed itself against the Word,
        Thus striving to rob God
    Of the dear Son, and of the Holy Ghost;
    Ignoring union of the great Jehovah
        With the Elder Brother,
And the Comforter, he promised.
Yet oft the voices of the three, the blessed trinity,
Proclaimed the Word, and human hearts thus helped
    and saved,
Gave honor to the Father, Son, and Holy Ghost,
    And so the Word prevailed.

Next papal power, the "man of sin," of which Paul
    speaks,
    Sought to "change times and laws."
    As ignorance prevailed, and gross corruption,
Superstition lifted up its hydra-head,
    And image-worship, and relics of the saints,
    And payment of large fees, which found their way

Into the treasuries of pope and cardinals,
>Who made the homage
Of their poor deluded victims
>A passport to the heavenly land.
>>And though God's Word
As seed was sown in many a human heart,
And in due time would grow and bring forth fruit,
Yet priestly pontiffs, with their councils and decrees,
>The power they claimed to pardon sin,
>And grant protection of the saints,
Took mighty hold upon the ignorant and weak,
Who gladly bowed their necks to " Romish yoke."
>But God, the loving Father, kept his own,
>And here and there, through all the earth,
Were found his true and earnest ones,
Fearless and faithful workers in the cause of truth,
And by their efforts many souls were gathered in
>Of such as should be saved.
And thus God's Word proved far more potent
Than that " Mystery of Sin," the Church of Rome.

Among the powers that oppose the Word,
>The human heart presents itself,

Full of deceit, and evil tempers, with proud will
>Ignoring God, his power, his Word,
>>Scoffing at sacred things;
Wrapping itself in pride and much conceit,
>Forgetting that the God they scorn
>>Could blast them with a breath,
And send them down to deeper, darker depths of woe,
>Than their vile hearts had e'er conceived.
But even here the Word has power.
>The loving invitation, "Come to me,"
The tender touch of hands once pierced,
>The cleansing blood on Calvary spilled,
Applied to hearts full of deceit and every deadly thing,
>Can so transform and cleanse,
>>That God, well pleased,
Will take and seal them as his own.

And thus, through all the centuries,
Christianity has been the leading power.
Taking in its train the noblest intellects,
>The science and the art of ages past;
And in its grand, triumphant, onward way,
>Each power to oppose shall be brought low,

Each foe destroyed, God's Word prevail,
Until the nations, dwelling in most distant climes,
  And in earth's darkest homes,
Shall know of God, his Son, the Christ who died for all;
  The Holy Ghost, God's messenger of peace
To such as hear his Word and love his name.

A Bridge of Years.

EIGHT years ago to-night they stood,
  The lover by his chosen bride,
    Within her childhood's home.
About them were the old familiar scenes
That almost seemed to her a part of life.
Dear friends, with saddened brows, were there,
  Yet smiling through their tears,
Rejoicing in their joy, and with them sympathizing
  In the hopes and fears, that found
    Within their hearts a resting place.
No anxious thought dwelt in the maiden's heart,
  For well she knew his loyal lips

Would never promise what the heart refused to yield.
   And he, in restful trust, believed
      Her love and tenderness
   Would smooth and beautify his life,
   Now they had met to consummate
      The vows made in the past.

Before them stood the man of God, with brow serene.
His earnest manner and his thrilling voice
      Impressed us in a solemn way,
        As with befitting words
   He made the "twain one flesh,"
Through weal or woe, in life or death;
A union recognized by God and angels,
To be annulled only by the close of time,
      The ending up of years.

Home voices now no longer lingered on their ears,
The kind farewells had all been uttered,
      The last look taken at the spot
Associated with each childish thought and prayer.
To the young wife that home was very dear,
For long ago a father's grave was made
      Beneath its shadowy trees;

A widowed mother lingered still; an only sister,
    Sharer of her thoughts and cares;
A brother, well beloved, formed ties as strong as life.

  With tearful eyes and aching heart
She turned away to seek another home
    With him she loved.
And hope, with cheery presence, lingered near;
  Beauty was all about them, for earth
Was radiant with her wealth of charms.
The low winds murmured in a joyous way;
The tall trees breathed a "God speed" as they passed;
    The rocks, piled high above them,
    Were reminders of the rock
  On which their feet were placed;
    For well they knew
    Their future was with Him
    " Who doeth all things well."
The calm blue waters of the peaceful lake
Spoke with prophetic voice of future rest;
    And these glad omens were gathered
In their inmost hearts, to be remembered
When their prophetic words had all been proved.

A little cottage, clothed in green and white,
    Was garnished for their use.
And, as on near approach, they caught a glimpse,
    It seemed to smile a welcome,
    And as they entered at its opened doors
The unspoken language of each heart was this,
" Thy people shall be mine, thy God my God."

Loving hearts encouraged loving hands
    To beautify this chosen spot,
Until, at last, the birds mistook it for their home.
And flowers climbed up and smiled
      Within the windows;
      And the glad winds
    Went roaming through the rooms,
      Murmuring their approbation.
      They labored diligently,
      And toil's reward was theirs.
Contentment dwelt within their home,
And peace, a welcome guest, has ne'er departed.
Morning and evening from the home altar
Has risen the sacrifice of grateful hearts
To him who daily blesses and sustains.

Years come and go, each shorter than the last,
　　Each filled to overflowing
With joyous memories of the past ;
　　　　With present happiness,
　　And blissful prospects of the future,
　　Where earthly joys, and charms
　　　　That satisfy in time,
Shall pale beside the brighter home,
And fuller life they each will share.

Moses at the Burning Bush.

O N Horeb's plain,
　　A shepherd, lingering, watched his flocks ;
　　And, when the pasturage grew poor,
He led them back, for fresher food, toward Sinai,
Which hid its rugged head within the clouds,
As if to watch their birth, and journeyings through
　　　　space ;
To learn the secrets of the dew and rain,
As they were lifted from the depths

To be again returned to bless the earth.
   The path by which the flocks were led
Had been untrodden hitherto,
For those who dwelt within the mountain's shadow,
Called it God's hiding place,
And out of fear, or reverence,
Refrained from coming near.
But Moses, who had dwelt in other lands,
Until in recent time he journeyed hither,
And found the land of Midian pleasant to his sight,
Had found a friend in Jethro, priest and patriarch of
   the land,
And took his flocks,
And, in his care for them, had wandered wide,
Not having heard the rumor that God's voice
Was sometimes heard
Echoing from out the mountain depths.
   And Moses tarried with his flocks,
Perhaps rehearsing all his wondrous past,
Or thinking of the promises of God, who loved his
   nation,
That were now in sore distress by reason of their bonds ;
The hardness of the hearts of those

Who made them drink the bitter waters of their
    servitude;
Thinking of the God,
To whom, in smaller measure, he might be akin ;
For those who cared for Moses in his youth
Proclaimed him " of a form divine," and of a "gener-
    ous mind."
And as he waxed strong in the faith—
With towering mountains pointing to the heavens,
And God so near—
He saw a wondrous sight ;
A bush on fire, yet unconsumed,
Though leaf and branch were wrapped in flame ;
And as he thought on near approach
To solve the wondrous mystery,
A voice came from the flame, and called him by his
    name,
And bade him draw not hither,
And did likewise say :
" Put off thy shoes from off thy feet,
The place whereon thou standest now is holy ground."
And still the voice made utterance:
" I am thy father's God,

I hear the cry that comes from out thy nation's heart.
Their sorrows are my own:
I come to bring them out of bonds;
Thee have I chosen as my instrument
To lead them to the promised land.
Do thou have courage, I will send thee to the king
With large demand for liberty for Israel's host."

       And Moses hid his face,
And dared not look on God,
And cried, "Who am I, Lord," and felt so self-abased,
Too humble for this mighty work.
And cried again, "O Lord, my Lord!
I am not eloquent, nor have been in the past,
Nor since thy words fell on my ears;
But I am slow of speech and slow of tongue;"
And Moses trembled, as he said, "I pray thee
Send by hand of him whom thou wilt send."

       And God made answer:
"Who hath made man's mouth,
Or who the dumb, or deaf, the seeing, or the blind?
I am hath sent you, *I* the *Lord.*
Now, therefore, go;
I will be with thee, with thy words,

And teach thee, as thou goest, what to say;
And Aaron, whom thou lovest,
Thy brother, shall go with thee—
He speaketh well; he cometh forth to meet thee now;
Speak thou to him, put words into his mouth—
He shall be mouth to thee.
And thou shalt be as God to him.
And take my rod, wherewith thou shalt do signs;
And go, return to Egypt—the men are dead that
     sought thy life."
     So Moses took his wife,
And took his sons, and took the rod of God,
And took a blessing from Jethro's lips,
Who said, "Go thou in peace."
And Moses went, and met his brother in the mount,
And kissed him, as he told the words and all the signs
Commanded of the Lord.
And then they went, Moses and Aaron,
To the elders of the tribes,
And spake the words the Lord had said.
And did the signs in sight of all the gathered hosts.
And they believed
That God had seen them in their darkest hour,

And heard their cry.
And all the people wept, and bowed their heads,
And worshiped Him
Who spake to Moses from the burning bush.

A Gracious Answer.

"Ask and ye shall receive."

THERE came in my life a Spring-time,
　　When the pulses of health ran low,
　And the tired hands were folded,
　　　The footsteps were weary and slow.

And my spirit was sad for the dear ones,
　　Who each tried to lift a part,
For the household burdens were heavy—
　　Heavier far was the pain at my heart.

And so I asked the dear Father,
　　To send me comfort and rest,
To watch over and bless the home fold,
　　In the way that seemed to him best.

I knew he remembered the lilies,
    To clothe them in beauty and grace ;
And the sparrows worth only a farthing,
    Have in his great heart a place.

And He, too, most surely has promised,
    Not a hair of our heads shall fall
To the ground without his knowledge,
    For his love reaches out over all.

And so as the time went drifting,
    There came to my home one day,
A friend, beloved and helpful,
    And she came with a purpose to stay

Till my tired frame grew stronger,
    And the sunken cheeks more bright,
Till the step should become elastic,
    And the eyes with hope alight.

And her very step was restful,
    As she moved with a quiet grace,
Her eyes as blue as the heavens,
    A comforting smile on her face.

12

And with tender touch she lingered,
    Wherever she most could aid;
And the voice of the dear Elder Brother,
    Was the voice she always obeyed.

And so through all of the Spring-time,
    Like a ministering spirit she went,
With supplies of grace for daily needs—
    Truly God a helper had sent.

And when the Summer with bloom and fruit,
    Came to bless our home with its cheer,
We felt that our friend we could not give up,
    For she seemed each day the more dear.

And still she tarried, the vintage to glean,
    And place with the Autumn store,
And health came slowly back to the home,
    Where sorrow had reigned before.

And when at last her mission was done,
    More precious to us than fine gold,
We knew that to her a richer reward,
    Would be meted in measure fourfold.

The Morning-Glory.

REST upon my couch
And watch the morning-glories
Twining along the porch.
Each separate plant seems eager
To outstrip its neighbor, as it upward climbs,
Lifting its wealth of bloom to loftier heights;
Its heart-shaped leaves are each a study,
With their wondrous tracery in silence wrought,
Each unlike the other,
Yet all of perfect handiwork.
The tiny tendrils, with graceful curves,
Reach forth, as if imploring sun and rain,
And bracing air
To grant new life and strength to root and stalk,
Giving each bell-shaped flower its varied hue,
As if a brush, dipped in the rainbow's surplus wealth,
Had sprinkled here and there
Choice bits of color.
From this dainty bit of nature's workmanship,
May I this lesson learn,

To climb from day to day, to loftier heights of faith,
And as each morn fresh beauty meets my eye,
 So may some word or act of mine,
 Shed brightness daily over other lives.

An Ideal Holiday.

CHILD.

WHAT would you like best, mother mine,
 This lovely morn in the sweet Spring-time?
 For a fairy whispered to me I might say
That mother should have what she wanted to-day.

MOTHER.

You may tell the fairy I'd like the best,
Freedom from care, a day of rest;
When the work would move itself along,
With a gentle tread like a restful song;

When the breakfast cloth would be neatly laid,
And the morning meal by deft fingers made;

When sweeping and dusting were out of sight,
Not a care would I have this day so bright.

CHILD.

And what would you do dear, mother mine,
If you had a whole day of precious time?
Would you read, or sing, or visit, or play,
Through all the long hours of a great long day?

MOTHER.

I would take my dear ones and speed away,
Where the grasses wave and the breezes play;
I would walk along 'mid the wildwood flowers,
And would seek for cool and shady bowers.

I would gather my arms full of treasures rare
(For nature has plenty and all may share,)
Of mosses and ferns and tangles of green,
As pretty a chaos as ever was seen.

I'd weave them in garlands so dainty and neat,
Or make them in clusters both pretty and sweet,
Or fashion in bracelets for fair dimpled arms,
Or girdles of green to enhance youthful charms.

I'd find a seat under shadowy leaves,
Where mosses are piled at the roots of old trees,
Where the squirrels play in their gayer moods,
Or gather nuts from the deeper woods.

I'd listen to songs of the dear little birds,
Who chatter and sing in musical words
Of the brightness in store for them all through the years,
Their homes and their loves, their hopes and their fears.

Of green leaves I'd make a dainty cool cup,
And fill with ripe berries piled up to the top;
They grow in the borders, close by the pure stream,
Wearing tasty red coats, but their cloaks are dark green.

The streamlet I'd follow as it ripples along,
With its murmur and trill and quaver of song,
Washing the pebbles and blessing the bloom,
That o'ershadows the banks, throwing forth rich perfume.

And so I would linger till setting of sun,
When long shadows warned me that day was done;
I would say to my dear ones when the birds seek their rest,
We'll hasten again to our own home-nest.

An Uninvited Guest.

SEED had fallen away by the kitchen-door; we did not know about it until a little plant thrust itself forth from the moist earth, and after looking about for a few days started out as if to investigate more fully. It seemed to be an energetic little thing, for in a short time it had found its way across the back yard, had climbed up, and was peeping between the white pickets, looking, we thought, at the mass of inwoven morning-glories, nasturtions, and sweet peas that shaded the porch. It was evidently pleased with the outlook, for after a little hesitation it climbed through and made its way along, not venturing to fasten itself to the frail cords that sufficed for the more dainty plants, but forming a base to the pretty screen that put on new beauties day by day.

The vine seemed to thrive, and as it had found its way in such quiet, unobtrusive fashion, we decided it might retain possession for a time at least.

And so each morning as we gave it friendly greeting we saw it had journeyed a little farther, and its green leaves had broadened. Its stalk had taken an added strength, and as if to make sure of its footing it had thrown out little tendrils here and there that wound themselves about the grasses or caught hold of the morning-glories with a tenacious grasp as if they did not mean to let go again.

And so it wandered on until it reached the broad door stone, looked up into the porch and on into the rooms as if speculating about taking possession. We watched the result with curious eyes, to find at last, that through advice of its kindly neighbors, or by its own superior wisdom, it had turned about, taking a wide circuit, possibly with the intention of returning again to its starting point, leaving, however, two or three great golden bell-shaped blossoms as a token of gratitude for kindly treatment it had received, or, perhaps, as security for rent. We are interested in the further movements of our "uninvited guest;" it has yet two or three months in which to pursue its wanderings before the Autumnal frosts shall cripple its powers. In the mean time its innate strength and unbounded ambition make its possibilities immense; we will try to wait patiently for their development.

The Baptism.

THE day had waned,
   Long shadows fell aslant the road o'er which we
      passed ;
   A pleasant country road,
With now and then a mossy bank on either side,
   Inviting to repose.
And little groves were scattered by the way,
   Among whose shadows one would love to sit.
Farther on a stately tree, like an untiring sentinel,
Looked forth o'er hill and dale, o'er distant lake and
      pretty little towns,
   Which, in the distance, seemed asleep,
While the great hills beyond kept guard above them,
   As a mother guards the slumbers of her little one.

As we pass the simple, country homes,
   Little maidens and their sisters,
   Gray-haired sires and tender mothers,
      Hasten along the path we tread.
Husbands and fathers join the throng,

With quiet expectation on each face,
　　For, at the sunset hour,
When all have met beside the cooling stream,
A solemn ordinance, like unto that which Christ
　　In Jordan's depths received,
That he might thus fulfill all righteousness,
　　Will be observed.
We pass along, listening to song of bird,
　To insect voices, and rippling waters,
　　Until we reach a limpid pool,
Roofed by an overhanging tree, festooned with vines.
Across the stream a sloping hill-side, with foliage
　　overhead,
And underneath are velvet moss and tufted mounds
　　Inwrought with scarlet berries.
　　　　Here and there, in graceful beauty,
Youth and age are grouped ;
The bright-eyed girl, with brown or golden tresses,
　　And the whitened locks of age,
Each one intent upon the solemn service of the hour.
　　　The sun had made
His royal march across the sky, and lingered now,
As if to look abroad o'er the fair earth,

Which grew and freshened day by day,
As sunbeams sought the quiet nooks and hiding-places
Where Mother Nature keeps her treasures,
And coaxed them forth to light and fragrance.
Now its rays touched vale and hill-top,
   Rested on the shimmering wave,
And bathed the faces of the waiting throng.

  Anon a gorgeous cavalcade
Came trooping up from northern skies,
As if the king of day had called his hosts together
  For a grand review ;
Their royal robes of crimson, gold, and purple,
Mingled with silver sheen, became them well.
  Strange and fantastic was the grouping,
Horses and chariots there were, and floating banners,
Whose reflected light was thrown far southward,
As signals to uncounted hosts
   To join the glittering pageant.
And one could almost fancy
That the dainty forms that hurried up from southward
  skies,
Had wings and harps beneath their tinted robes,

Perchance had come from neighboring worlds
To view the scene
         O'er which the angels might rejoice,
And carry back to other hosts the news,
     "The dead's alive, the lost is found."

     A solemn silence crept o'er all the place,
     Even nature's voices hushed themselves,
   As the pure man ordained of God stepped forth,
   His brow aglow with living light, and prayed
A simple, fervent prayer that must have reached the
     ear of Him
Who dwells on high.
A hymn was sung
    Whose echoes reached across the vale,
As when the Law was read to Israel's host,
And borne from Ebal's slopes to fruitful Gerizim.

A wife and mother, who had vowed to live for Christ,
And train her children in the living way,
   Walked calmly down the bank,
And, in the name of Father, Son, and Holy Ghost,
     Was there baptized.
Next came a maiden, who had sought and found

The " Pearl of Price;"
And, as the waters laved the yielding form,
　　Thoughts of the mother who had gone before.
Leaving the orphaned one to find the cross
　　Without her hand to guide,
Filled many a heart, and prayers were breathed that she
　　　　might
Always pray as now: " Father, be thou my Guide;
In youth, my helper, in maturer years, forsake me not;
　　And, when the hour of death shall come,
　　Accept and save by merit of thy Son."

We bowed our heads for final words of blessing,
Just as the sun went down behind the western hills;
And turned to seek our homes,
　　Feeling that Christ in God was honored,
　　　　And that the dove, the Holy Ghost,
That hovered over Jordan's wave,
　　　　　　Had been with us,
And left its impress on our hearts.

Nettie.

I.

MAIDEN beloved in your morning of years,
I watch you to-day through happy tears,
As your feet are poised on the threshold of days,
And you look abroad o'er life's untrodden maze.

You are all too frail for the battle and strife,
For friction must come into every life;
Your tender heart would sorrow each day,
For trials are strewn o'er each step of the way.

But you charm with your dainty winsome face,
With your witching ways and baby grace,
With the tender look to your dark eyes given,
As if borrowed from out the treasures of heaven.

There's a rest in the touch of your dimpled hand,
Like a hallowed touch from the better land;
The words that you lisp as they fall on our ear,
Are like the music that in dreams we hear.

O my precious treasure, my white pearl so fair,
With your glossy ringlets of raven hair,

Could I know that you might always walk by my side,
I am sure that my heart in peace would abide.

Your footsteps I'd watch with tenderest care,
Each day of your life should be hallowed by prayer,
My own hands should pluck every thorn from your way,
Should the loving Father permit you to stay.

II.

O maiden beloved of the tender years,
I see you again through blinding tears,
For your weary feet on the threshold stand,
Of the open door of the heavenly land.

Your beautiful life is almost o'er,
You hear the tones from the farther shore;
Voices like music fall on your ear,
Heavenly voices which we may not hear.

Your angel wings are plumed for the flight,
Your face is veiled in a halo of light;
The tender gleam of your wonderful eyes
Speaks to our hearts of your pleased surprise.

A touch, a caress, our birdling has flown,
The Savior has come and called for his own;
She has left the threshold, the struggle is o'er,
The angels have closed the open door.

And now the dear feet will journey along,
Through pleasant paths in the land of song,
And the angels who her way shall guide
Are the friends who before her passed over the tide.

O fathers and mothers, dear friends that are gone,
Will you tenderly watch o'er our angel one?
Will you tell her we love her, and truly will come
To our mansions and hers in that beautiful home?

The three little years that she journeyed through time
Were like silvery streamlets that through Eden twine,
Bringing freshness and beauty to bank, vale, and flower,
So blest was our Eden by this transplanted flower.

Lines.

Lines.

SUGGESTED BY THE DEATH OF A YOUNG MAN WHILE ATTENDING SCHOOL.

GLANCING backward through the years,
A picture rare reveals itself; a home
Where God is loved and honored, among
Its brightest ornaments, a darling son.
Parental hearts beat proudly as they look
Upon his promise, while his future is
To them a beacon, shedding light and warmth
O'er their declining years.
A loving sister shared his childish sports,
Grieving when he grieved, and in his joys
Rejoicing, while without stint they lavished
Each upon the other a wealth of love,
Their thoughts and tastes so interwoven,
Reminding one of oak and clinging vine.

There came a time
When thoughts of God, his claims, man's sinfulness,
God's wondrous love, impressed his heart, and,
Listening to the "still small voice," he hastened

13

To the cross, and gave himself without
Reserve to God.

In all the past no
Vulgar word had soiled his lips, no mark of
Sin was on his brow. But now the Savior
Was his best and dearest friend, and by his
Side he walked and nothing feared.
In prime and vigor he went forth
Where many congregate, who love to drink
At learning's fount. Ambitious, earnest,
He girded close his armor, and strove
To fit himself for life's great warfare.
Friends rallied to his side, and teachers
Proudly pointed to the height which he thus
Early had attained.

Too soon sad tidings came
To friends. Disease had fastened on that
Manly form, and agonized, he prayed
For home. His friend, one tried and trusted,
Nursed him tenderly, relieving every want
With thoughtful care. Parents and sister
Hastened to his side, with tender touch,
And all the helps that gold could bring.

But vain all efforts.
The prayers and tears, the cries of those
Who loved him best were powerless to save.
Now and then there came a moment
When he knew the dear home faces; and as
In childhood, folded safe within his
Mother's arms, he said "Our Father," so when
Near the close of life, he laid his head
Upon that mother's breast,and breathed the prayer
First sanctified by holiest lips.
Dear ones went with him to the river's brink,
And, as he neared the other shore, they seemed
To hear his glad voice shouting back,
"Forever with the Lord!"

A mourning group stand watching for the train
To bring the form so loved in life; and while
We waiting prayed that God would "bind the
Broken hearts," the dreaded moment came.
A band of youthful students
Gathered round the coffined form.   With tear-wet
Eyes and measured tread, they bore him to the
Hearse.   Gladly would friends apply the only

Balm to aching hearts; but words have little   -
Power when soul and brain are paralyzed
With grief.

      Sadly we pass within the home
So late the abode of peace.   But now
The angel folds her wings, while one of dark,
Forbidding mien usurps her place, and for
The time bears rule, presenting to each lip
A bitter cup, which must be drained down to
Its very dregs.
        Tears, groans, and prayers
Now echo forth the grief too deep for words.
O death! relentless! why point your arrow
At the young, the gifted, and the pure?

      But God is here,
And while the voice of prayer is heard above
The anguish, our faith looks forth to the "blest
Mansions," where the freed spirit dwells.
      O precious trust,
That teaches us to place our hands within
The hand that chastens, and helps to say, "He
Doeth all things well."

For eighteen years he dwelt on earth—
Eighteen short years, and yet how full
Of precious memories; how rich in their
Results, with life work better met than many
A one who counts his fourscore years.
Oh, let us reverently thank God, who
"Gave and took again."
We know that classmates promised by his side
To seek the Lord, and time has proved those vows
Were true. And so we know that we shall see
Him decked with starry crown when we, too, reach
The shining shore.

O mourning ones, rejoice. The eyes now closed
To you have pierced the veil, and feast upon
The glories hid from mortal sight. The feet,
For whose glad coming now you may not look
Are walking o'er the "golden streets." The hands,
Whose ministry you loved, have found a harp
Of gold, while voice and lip unite in songs
Of praise to Him who conquered death.

My Pen and I

DEAR little pen, we have been friends together,
  We've traveled over many a snowy plain;
Through all the long days of this Summer weather,
We've found far more of pleasure than of pain.

We've wandered out among the dewy grasses,
And rested 'neath the friendly grape-vine's shade,
Have roamed among the wild wood mosses,
In thickets where the birds their nests have made.

Together we have climbed the lofty mountains,
And from their heights have looked o'er all the land;
Or slaked our thirst from out the hidden fountains,
Or stood upon the grand old ocean's strand.

We've drifted northward to the arctic winters,
Or tarried under burning torrid skies;
Or southward, helped by favoring breezes,
Where strange new beauties met our waiting eyes.

We've sought the heavens, and looked on old Orion,
The mighty warrior with his belt and sword,

Who treads his beat like sentinel untiring,
Worthy of mention in God's holy Word.

The " Pleiads" we have seen in near communion,
Seven sisters in one household, loving kind,
And often wondered if, in pleasant union,
They sang together in the " morn of time."

We've looked into the hidden depths of ocean,
Quiet and restful under God's command ;
Again we've seen the waves in wild commotion,
Yet knew he held the waters in his hand.

We've wandered out, while yet the stars were shining,
And watched the shadows as they fled away;
We've gladly welcomed the first hint of morning,
That promised us another precious day.

We've seen the great gray eastern walls dissolving,
As sun rays climbed aloft with rosy hue,
Revealing earth in daintiest adorning
Of gossamer and pearly drops of dew.

We've watched the sun, marching in stately grandeur,
Until half-way across the vaulted dome,

Throwing its rays about in lavish manner,
Blessing the earth from north to southern zone.

We've seen it set in such a wondrous glory,
That lip, or voice, or pen can not describe;
Perhaps an angel's brush might tell the story;
We thought the "golden gates" were opened wide.

Together we have read the precious pages,
A revelation of God's wondrous plan,
Surpassing all the wisdom of the sages,
Lifting to high estate poor fallen man.

We've found the spoken words and thoughts of Jesus,
Among all other helps, by far the best.
We've borne in mind the loving invitation,
"Come unto me, and I will give you rest."

We've proved the truth, the word of Christ unbroken,
"My peace with you shall ever more remain."
We'll trust him for the later promise spoken,
"I go, but will return for you again."